DIE RICH

by

M.H. VESSEUR

DIE RICH

A Radio Detective

A novel by
M.H. Vesseur

Vibes Publishing

Published by Vibes
www.mhvesseur.com
www.facebook.com/MHVesseur

Second edition
ISBN 978-94-91908-38-5 (paperback, 2nd edition)
ISBN 978-90-806920-4-6 (epub with DRM)

Die Rich

One

Death can look beautiful if it wants to. It's really not such a big deal. It will simply take on one of its sympathetic disguises and fool you. One of the oldest disguises is of course the sea: it has been around longer than anyone can remember and it never fails to entertain your senses. At any given moment a million people may be watching some oceanic view below a setting sun, the water sparkling with golden drops as if it were on fire. Slowly, day after day, this spectacular sight moves around the globe, aweing mankind, and most of us will be fooled by the artistry of death's façade.

Carl Pappas was dead in the water and he could not help pondering about the beauty of the ocean surrounding him and the sharp contrast with the hopelessness of his situation.

I am freezing and growing numb in the water, he thought, and all I can do is look at Vincent van Gogh's amazing starry night.

A warm yellow light was emanating from the mainland several miles away from him, aspiraling into the sky above, where it was welcomed by a sea of stars. This whole oil painting feast was then mirrored into the ocean's surface, and given a slight twist. There were hardly any waves, so much of the mirrored view remained untouched, stretching or shrinking slightly with the passing of a wave. Pappas tried to remember if he had ever seen a better view, but nothing emerged from the depths of his mind.

Soon my strength will have ebbed from my arms and legs and I'll no longer be able to swim. Then this accursed Van Gogh painting will simply swallow me whole, he thought.

With his lips, blue from the cold, he mumbled the sentences he thought up, as if he were close to his real microphone, the trusted SM7, as if he were speaking directly to the millions of listeners of his daily radio show The Boardroom. However precarious his position, Carl Pappas remained the world's number one bizz jockey under all circumstances. If only he could come up with some relevant remark to make this whole drowning thing interesting for the international business community! Of course he could create a special show about saving your life when your corporate jet plunges into the ocean, or your private yacht sinks within eyesight of the harbor of some offshore tax haven you happen to be visiting.

Turning the whole thing into a fine radio moment would be a sinch. It was the surviving part that worried Carl Pappas. There was no way he was going to swim all the way to the shore. His physical condition would simply not allow that to happen. And as long as it was dark not a single soul would spot him here.

"OK people," he said aloud, attempting to revive himself from becoming drowsy. "OK. Uhhh..."

He needed a few moments to get into it.

"Men and women of the business, welcome to The Boardroom, where just like any other day we ask ourselves: where do we stand? If you know the answer, you may call now. But don't take this lightly; many went before you. Many were mistaken. And are grounded now, in court, in jail or in hell, or, like me, dead in the water. No matter if you're a CEO or a secretary, just send your corporate chopper *right now* and have me picked up before my voice goes dead and WCBN will have to cancel the rest of tonight's show. That'd be a real pity considering we have some great guests lined up for you peo..."

Carl Pappas, the bizz jockey, stopped speaking in mid sentence as some water gulfed into his open mouth. It was salt as hell. He swallowed it. Then he engaged in a coughing fit.

After a few moments he looked away from the shore again, trying to find the small island that he had come from earlier in the evening. It was nowhere to be seen in the thick darkness. There was a starry night in that direction too, but no warm light coming from a city; just a black hole that represented the ocean.

He thought: way to go, Pappas.

He felt his jaw. It was still hurting from the blow he had received. He thought of some other injuries he had sustained in the past twenty-four hours, some nasty cuts, but he felt nothing. He had escaped and through some miracle survived this far. Now his pocket full of miracles appeared to be empty.

Carl Pappas, the bizz jockey, currently not on the air, looked around again, suddenly anxious to see if any of the people who had done this to him were looking for him. There were no boats, neither within visual range nor within earshot.

Then he sighed deep and started singing softly the only song in the universe that made any sense to him right now: "With a little luck, we can work it out..."

Well, he thought, at least I am *not* going to die rich.

So, he knew the end. He did not even want to start thinking about how he got to this ending in the first place.

Two

It had been Hitomi's idea, for starters. Carl Pappas, the bizz jockey, was never really interested in the super rich as a class — he tried to maintain a strictly neutral position when people's assets were concerned.

"Don't emphasize something you don't want to emphasize," he said when his producer suggested the topic in the weekly editorial meeting.

But Hitomi Sakamoto was not impressed. It must be said she was a master at keeping a straight face. It would take a truckload of unsettling information for her to move a facial muscle. A school of sumo wrestlers might do the trick, but nothing less. She was not an easy person to impress or to put off. She consumed hardly any coffee, she scarcely drank and she didn't smoke. There was not much fun to be had in the company of Hitomi, who spent her off time either in the gym or running through a park or along the riverside through the heart of the city. She was in her forties but she was in great shape and maintained a level of energy and focus unparalleled at WCBN — even by their boss Phil Solo, who was no sissy when it came to energy and focus.

"The super rich amount to something like one percent of the world's population and they possess something like thirty-nine percent of the world's private wealth. There is no way the number one business talk show is going to continue avoiding that," Hitomi said and she said it so fast that no one in the room had a chance to interrupt. "And I fail to see how inviting a couple of super rich fathers and their sons to the show and chat about how they deal with their riches, equals emphasizing."

"Is there a mike open in this room? I'm hearing the word 'emphasize' echoing time and time again," snapped Phil Solo, the boss of WCBN Radio. He looked his usual confident self: the man who could have been in a Gucci ad when he was younger. The man who could be a movie star because he resembled one, though no one could ever come up with a name. The man who wore suits that made statements before he even opened his mouth. Solo was making one of his unexpected surprise visits to the editorial meeting. This usually happened only if he wanted to inject some new ideas into the show as if he were a team member rather than the boss. The boss' ideas would, of course, be rejected by Carl himself at all times without a second thought, so being in a routine meeting was the only chance for Phil to suggest anything. And the man did this so expertly that no one in the room would be able to tell afterwards what ideas Phil Solo had actually planted in the team members' heads.

But he remained a nuisance nevertheless.

"I'm all for kicking rich ass," said Job Messner, the writer-reporter who had been on the team since the beginning and was mainly responsible for writing soundbites on complicated topics. Even though Carl Pappas was an experienced improviser when it came to making jokes and one of the finest business connoisseurs on the planet, he could not ad lib all machinations of the worldwide corporations. There was always the risk of losing the audience in an elaborate explanation. Or the risk of making nasty mistakes. It was Messner's job to mash things up till Carl could squeeze them into one breath. He was a soft spoken man in a 1970s teachers outfit, sort of brownish, worn, out of time, with matching wild curly hairs. "But I do have a problem with the numbers you're presenting here, Hitomi. You cannot simply speak of the super rich without giving some parameters. How rich is somebody supposed to be exactly before they qualify?"

"It's human interest, for God's sake," yelled Hitomi, still not changing her facial expression. "I can see Carl creating a fine table talk with fathers and sons about power and money and about the old generation letting go and allowing the kids to bring their own ideas. It can be fascinating. It's not about money, it's about what money does to people."

"If anyone can pull it off, it's Carl," Phil agreed. "Mind you, I'm not saying I necessarily like it. I mean it's going to cost a lot of time — and thus money — to get some rich families to agree to be on the show. And then our BJ will probably piss some of them off. And then my ass will be on the line again, as usual. But it can be powerhouse radio. There'll be a lot of attention. A lot of people pickin' up the phone. What do you think?"

Carl started pacing the room. The team sat and waited. They knew the ritual. The bizz jockey didn't like the editorial stuff. He was a live radio hero. That's when he became everybody's favorite guy. That's when he became a shark, a cheetah and a man on the moon all at the same time. But he also knew that the work of his team was a crucial preparation for his Olympic achievement: the gluing of ten million worldwide listeners to their radios.

"We have to be careful about this. I do not want to attack people for their riches. I don't care how much money a guest has accumulated through the years. My show is about business responsibility. If there's the slightest doubt about my political stance, I'll lose part of my audience. Soon as someone over at CNN or Radio Dubai starts calling me a lefty, I'm in trouble."

He looked at Job Messner. "You have to come up with a shitload of soundbites for me to throw in and keep me away from the personal wealth issue. I'm willing to attack anyone in my show and push them to the limit, but won't attack anyone for being rich."

"You're such a liar," said Solo. "I'm rich as hell and you're picking on me all the time."

They all laughed and shouted abuse. It was a chicken run. But it was a good start. At least one show was on track now. Four more to go.

Five shows a week — what a job.

Three

The whole studio was in an uproar. It wasn't the guests so much as their entourage. The four men who were invited to sit at the large table during this evening's broadcast of The Boardroom were quiet. But swarming around them were their security personnel and staff and personal secretaries. And one hairdresser, a thin, affectionate man, exuberantly dressed in some pink outfit with lots of loose ends. He was standing by a chair, arranging one of the guest's hair. Carl Pappas made an entrance, saw the tableau and said for all to hear: "What's with the hair fetish?"

There was an awkward silence for a moment.

"Look at me!" said Carl. "A radiohead will do just fine."

"There's more to radio than meets the ear," snapped the hairdresser. "Don't you do something to feel good about yourself before you go live?"

"I shout abuse at the people close to me," said Pappas. "And as long as the ratings are high I get away with it."

"We're done anyway," said the guest whose hair was being done. He was a man in his early twenties, impeccably dressed in some shining suit that must've come straight from some exclusive atelier with a fancy name, his nails so thoroughly done that they shone even in this sublit environment. He got up from his chair and shook Carl's hand. "I'm William Hackensack the third, heir to the family business my father is..."

"What he's trying to say, Mr. Pappas," said a man who appeared to be an older version of Hackensack the third. The same exclusive suit, the same embalmed hands, the same careful pronunciation. "is that he's my oldest son and that he may one day share the responsibility of Hackensack Oil with his two brothers. But since he's already involved in the business it's likely he will assume a leading position, I guess. I'm the second Hackensack, by the way. Nice to meet you, sir. I'm Bill."

More handshakes. These were intimidating men, who took center stage immediately without even the slightest visible effort. Additionally, they had the looks of regular Vogue models.

"So where's the first Hackensack at?" Carl replied. This created exactly the kind of confusion he was after. Part of his success as the world's number one bizz jockey was his long list of golden rules. One of these golden rules was: *Every man's a captain, so there's gonna be a fight before the ship can leave the harbor.*

Father and son Hackensack looked at one another in mild confusion, which gave the team the opportunity to proceed.

"Carl, meet Rog Afficionades and his son Moon," said Hitomi Sakamoto without raising her voice. She made one of her trademark gestures towards the two other guests, an elegant wave with a hand that could have been designed by an original Geisha. Hitomi moved like a work of art.

"Nice to meet you folks," said Carl, shaking the hands of two man who, much unlike the Hackensacks, seemed to have nothing in common. The father, Rog, was obviously an old hippie, with hair like a haystack and a jeans outfit that was apparently stolen from a Woodstock memorabilia exhibition. Had the man been introduced as a member of Crosby, Stills, Nash & Young no one in the room would have been surprised.

The fact that the next guy he shook hands with, Moon, was actually Rog's son, was really the unbelievable part. Here stood a guy in his early twenties or late teens, dressed in a camouflage uniform, sporting a Ray-Ban that mirrored his surroundings and a hairdo that needed little attention: all hairs were greased to the brim and folded backwards in military unity. The kid sure had his name from the Summer of Love, but nothing else.

"It's an honor to be on your show," said Moon Afficionades, who unexpectedly turned out to be the most civilized of the men. Perhaps that had something to do with the presence of his mother, a pale beauty of a certain age who obviously deemed all botoxing and face lifting entirely unnecessary. She was dressed in lemon as if she were going to the beach, covered in all kinds of necklaces with Buddha's and various other flower power symbols.

"Thát is putting it mildly," she laughed, embracing Pappas faster than he could retread. "I am thrilled to be in close contact with a man who is not afraid to tell the Chinese chairman or the U.S. president or the Russian head of intimidation or some Arab emir how he feels about them and then have a row with the I.M.F. boss."

"Mrs. Afficionades, Carl," said Hitomi.

"Ah, you are the mother of Moon!" said Carl with a loud voice.

"Indeed."

"Not many women of successful business men are still around when the kids hit twenty," said Pappas for all to hear. "In your case I'm not surprised."

"Well Mr. Pappas," laughed Mrs. Afficionades, "you turn out to be exactly the charmer you appear on the radio. Do call me Rhiannon."

Carl sort of freed himself from her embrace right before it started to raise attention. "Rhiannon... wasn't she a fairy princess?"

"Yes. But we're here to let the men talk, so we'll have to get into that some other time, Carl," said Mrs. Afficionades.

Now there was giggling. Two girls in their late teens stood somewhere in the back, obviously connected to some of the men. They were dressed as if they were going to go on a catwalk any minute, and they looked at Carl in a way that he had learned to understand through the years — it was the kind of look that women reserve for men who are attractive because of their status. Some women are groupies by nature; they'll do anything for a close encounter with somebody famous. He had learned to consider himself a lucky guy, for he was oblivious to that sort of seduction. It left him cold. Carl Pappas was the sort of man who was solely interested in a woman if she fell for him, not for his fame. These girls were in their prime, but their adulation meant nothing to him. No hot sex with trophy hunting girls for the bizz jockey. No Sir.

"All right people, glad you could make it. Hitomi Sakamoto,

our producer, and between you and me the real architect of this show, is going to go through the schedule with you folks. I will not be talking to you other than the last moments before we go live, just to get the feel of things. I need to be spontaneous so I'm leaving you in the caring hands of Hitomi. And the hairdresser. Oh and everybody who is not in the broadcast is supposed to go to the room over there and sit behind the glass. Starting now. Thank you."

Carl turned around and left the room. A man in a suit with greying hair and the whitest teeth appeared from nowhere and accompanied him through the corridor leading away from the studio.

"Mr. Pappas I'm representing Mr. and Mr. Hackensack. My name is Barwinkle, I'm a lawyer and I need to make a few things clear before the show starts and I need you to sign for that."

Right around the first corner Carl stopped in mid-stride. "Sign? You got a picture?"

"A picture? You mean, like an ID?"

"No, not an ID. A photograph. You want my autograph, I'll need a picture."

"Mr. Pappas, you misunderstood me. I got some legal documents that need to be signed before..."

Carl Pappas, the bizz jockey, turned and resumed his course through the corridor. "Oh no, I don't do that sort of signing. You must go and see Phil Solo, he's the boss, he signs stuff. See you, mister."

In his office many floors above the studio Carl sat down behind his desk. There was a pile of paper, neatly stacked right before him. He had read it all before. He knew what he needed to know for the show. On top of the pile was one sheet filled with short notes. He read them. There was a short list of figures he looked at. He was astounded, just like the first time.

These people are indeed super rich, he thought. They did not get this far without certain characteristics that normal people don't have. What characteristics are they?

I need to kick ass to expose some truth here, he thought. "Gimme Some Truth" sounded in his head, one of his favorite songs he used to boost his morale with before engaging on this lunacy called The Boardroom. Gimme some truth, you mothers!

Four

Hitomi Sakamoto uttered a silent sigh of relief when the opening tune sounded and tonight's show got started. It had been a busy day, getting the last obstacles out of the way for four of the richest people on the planet. There had been lawyer's stuff. There had been tough questions. They had asked for a guarantee, a guarantee that Carl Pappas would make them look good. Of course they weren't gettin' it, but they were experts at raising hell, and that was exactly what they had been doing for days.

She had survived all that — and now The Boardroom was on the way.

The voice of WCBN Radio blasted from the sound system above the window beyond the console of the show's sound engineer Don Wozniak, the technician living in clothes that were too small for his puffed body. He was at home in this indoor environment, where he could toss his empty soda cans over his shoulders and where he could leave his pitch black hair sticking greasily in all directions and where he could see how long he could skip cleaning his huge glasses before Hitomi started making comments. Comments like: "Clean your filthy Thunderbirds glasses, Don Lech Wozniak!" To which he would then reply: "I don't have to. I can still see it's you, Hitomi." Or he would simply put "Passion" by Rod Steward through the speakers, loud and clear.

In spite of his shabby looks and his apparent chaotic way of working he was alert like no one else, as the show's introduction progressed and the anonymous WCBN Radio voice announced: "It's eleven o'clock. The city is dark, but the fire burns. It burns in the offices. It burns on Wall Street. It burns in the City. It burns on the Bund. It burns in Dubai. It burns in the factories and power plants. And it burns within us. Because we are the business and we all need redemption. This is the hour of delusion and today's truth. This is The Boardroom. Here is your prophet, the buddy and the bodyguard of every CEO, the Don Juan of every business babe. Here is the world's one and only bizz jockey. Here is your BJ: Carl Pappas!"

When the voice of Pappas took over from the anonymous WCBN speaker his words sounded like they were simply copied and pasted from a recording made on any other workday at this hour. In the early years of his radio show The Boardroom Carl had experimented with many different ways to open the show, but by now he had found his voice and, what's more, his audience liked this opening just fine. So he used the same words almost every day and only made minor changes, very seldomly. He did try out a different tone every day though, shifting emphasis from one word to another. One of his philosophies was that sometimes it was not what you said, but how you said it.

"Men and women of the business, welcome to The

Boardroom, where just like any other day we ask ourselves: where do we stand? If you know the answer, you may call now. But don't take this lightly; many went before you. Many were mistaken. And are grounded now, in court, in jail or in hell. A few moments from now I will introduce tonight's guests, who are already sweating on the other side of the microphone. But first... And yes, we have our first caller. This is Carl Pappas in The Boardroom, can I help you?"

"Hi this is Gyorgy."

"Well hello Gyorgy, where are you exactly?" said the bizz jockey.

"I'm in Dubai right now, but my business is in Budapest."

"You in the tower?"

"You mean the Burj Khalifa?"

Carl chuckled. "Of course I mean the Burj Khalifa. Please don't make a fool of yourself, Gyorgy. The listeners of this show are quite familiar with Dubai. What you up to in Dubai?"

"We build movable hotels for temporary workers, say on the premises of a building site of a nuclear plant. We can house up to ten thousand workers and as soon as the project is finished we move the whole container based setup to another part of the world."

"Nice accent you got there, Gyorgy. Am I getting this right, you house all these migrant workers who come from poor countries to work their poor butts off in some rich country, don't see their families for a whole year and are then sent home again without a pension with a back problem or a miner's lung? Are these the people you are referring to?" Carl sounded slightly agitated, but his audience was used to this by now. They probably thought he may as well be playacting anyway. That was all part of The Boardroom: push and shove.

"You're putting things in the wrong perspective here, Mr. Pappas," said Gyorgy. "They need the work and the income. And where they used to be housed in tents and filthy tenements they are now comfortable in cabins with private space and a kitchen and recreation. I don't see that as exploitation. I'm on the move all the time myself. Maybe you're just a socialist, Mr. Pappas?"

"You don't have to be a socialist to be worrying about the growing migrant working class of this world. Everybody's a migrant these days and that's fine when you're young but once you want to start a family it sucks. You can't raise kids when you are off to Dubai all the time."

From behind the window Hitomi Sakamoto made her typical gesture: she raised her hand like a pistol and blew imaginary smoke from the imaginary barrel. This was a sign for the bizz jockey to kill the topic and get to the point.

"It's a worldwide economy today, Mr. Pappas. It can't be changed simply because one disagrees."

"You got a point there, Gyorgy. Listen, you got a question to ask?"

"Yes, I got this problem with markets that are inaccessible. In certain areas of the world we might get a lot of business if we only engage more enthusiastically in a personal way."

"Can you, like, explain that Gyorgy? You're not making sense."

"My competitors bribe their way into the market. Sometimes it's just, you know, expensive dinners and brothels and stuff. Sometimes it's a lot of money or cars. Should I... I mean, I need to expand. My sales people disagree on the matter, it's a divisive thing."

"Thanks for your honesty, Gyorgy. I need you to be strong here. Can you do that? For me? For all of us?"

"Uh... well... I..."

"Corruption and clientelism are very, very bad for business. Honest competition revs up innovation and makes things more efficient. Without that we end up like East Germany in its last days: an old man with arteriosclerosis. The best man should get the contract, not the man with the contacts and the trickery. Now do us all a favor and say no to the thing. Plus make sure you report any attempt at bribery to the United Nations. They have some kind of task force for this sort of thing."

"How does that help me?"

"You figure that one out, Gyorgy. Help make this world a better place and be proud of it. Or to hell with it all and make an extra buck, but just remember this: you leave this world to your kids either a better place or a worse place, but you will leave it. Bye Gyorgy. Take care."

With a cutthroat gesture from Carl, Gyorgy was cut off.

"Another business soul saved, I hope," said the bizz jockey. "I know it hurts to lose business as a result of being honest. But hey... consider the alternative. So it's thumbs up for Gyorgy and on to some messages from our sponsors. After that we'll be talking about the other end of business, the place where you guys and dolls will all be when the dough is in. The place where you will be filthy rich. Once you get to that promised land you find out that it's not all a path of roses. There's a couple of thorns there as well. So stay tuned. This is Carl Pappas. This is WCBN Radio. This is The Boardroom."

Behind the window, as Hitomi checked the clock now that the show had been kicked off successfully, Don Wozniak pressed some screen buttons and leaned back.

"There's a guy and a girl in the corporate gym," he said to Hitomi.

"Please no," said Hitomi.

But Don commenced, unmoved. "The guy is lifting some serious weight. Right? He's all sweaty. He pauses and looks at the girl. 'You're not sweating,' he says. 'If you're not sweating, you're not really trying hard enough.' She pauses to look who's talking. He says: 'I can make you sweat.' The girl pauses again, looks him up and down with a look of utter contempt and says: 'The only way you are going to make me sweat is by giving me the flu.'"

Don looked at Hitomi triumphantly. Usually she was unimpressed with any of his jokes, but this time she was speechless. She looked at him for a moment. Then she recomposed herself.

"This is a remarkable moment, Don Lech Wozniak," she said. "You actually just tried to make a women friendly joke."

Don smiled. Behind that smile he was contemplating the options. Either Hitomi was really going to make him a compliment — a compliment from Hitomi was a rare pleasure for him — or she was going to give him a beating.

"And failed on both counts."

"Both counts?" said Don.

"It's not women friendly and it's also not funny. This girl's not laughing, see?" Then she walked out of the sound engineer's booth to check on Carl and his guests.

Don mimicked Hitomi's face and mouth: "This girl's not laughing," he said without making a sound.

Five

"Here we are again, people, and tonight's topic needs a firm introduction. Personally I need you to listen good. I don't care about who's rich and who's poor. In The Boardroom we're all equal. You may be some young kid pitching a start-up. You may be an old geezer after his third bankruptcy who spent last night under a bridge but is still ready to go with a new idea. You may be the heir to a family fortune or a Silicon Valley millionaire. Read my lips: I do not care. This is a business talk show. So we talk about the business of being rich tonight."

Carl Pappas moved his hand in the air and Don Wozniak ran a tune. It was a three note melody performed by a couple of trumpet players. Everybody in the room suddenly sat up straight. They'd been waiting for this.

"Tonight's topic is family riches. Or to be more precise: filthy riches. Obnoxious, over the top, coming right out of your ears wealth. You're swimming in it. You got way too much. It's overkill all the way. You can buy anything you want. And then put it in a museum and buy it again. How do you deal with that?"

From beyond the window a lot of people were watching. More than on most other nights. There were of course sound engineer Don Wozniak and producer Hitomi Sakamoto in the control room. There were members of the editorial staff in the viewing room, accompanying several relatives of the guests: wives, children, mothers, security personnel and one unknown woman who talked Russian and was probably a mistress of one of the guests, at least in the world according to Don Wozniak.

Carl didn't wait for an answer, but proceeded right away: "Let's dive right in, people. We got a lot of guests tonight but little time, so suffice it to say that we got two fathers with huge business and family fortunes — we're talking Bill Gates fortunes here, which reminds me that when I was young an Onassis fortune was all you needed. Plus you'd get Maria Callas and Jacqueline Kennedy thrown in as a bonus. We got the guys from Hackensack Oil here and the guys from Afficionades Media. I'm not sure what makes more money: oil or copyrights, but that's not the point. First on the mike is dad Hackensack. Bill, how do you know your son actually loves you? What if he's just sliming his way to his inheritance or to his chair in the board of your company?"

"You do go straight for the jugular, Carl," smiled Bill Hackensack. "But I guess we've all come to expect that from you. If you want facts, I can't give them to you. You can't measure love. I believe my son is not that kind of an actor, but of course I can't tell for sure. I guess it will come to light as soon as I'm dead."

"Did you love your own father, who left the business to you, or did you just make him believe that you did?" said the bizz jockey, fast and with a rasping voice for effect.

There was a moment of silence. Don moved his hand towards a button, just in case, and Hitomi's eyes enlarged.

Then Bill Hackensack laughed out loud. "The last thing in the whole world my old man cared about was whether I loved him or not. So it wouldn't have mattered either way."

"Come on, Bill, you can do better than that. If he knew you hated him, that would have changed things a bit, now wouldn't it? I repeat my question: did or did you not play the part of the loving son?"

"I looked up to my old man, he was all power and knowledge and dedication to the business. My mother was very supportive of that..."

They all looked up to see who was yawning loudly into the microphone, only to find out that it was the host. The bizz jockey interrupted the second Hackensack with a noise that was unforgiving.

"Funny how the powers that be always think they can avoid the issue at hand. You're talking around the issue here, Bill. So let's turn to your son, the third Hackensack. William. You're dad's buddy or what?"

"As long as my father believes that, we're up and running," chuckled William. "The oil business is more important than relationships. It has been in the family for a hundred years and next generations should be able to profit from it regardless whether grandpa got along with his dad. If you don't get along, work on it."

"Now we're getting somewhere," said Carl. "Basically you're saying you don't consider your dad your best friend. You just want him to pass on the family business and fortune to you. You're willing to play along with anything. Did you guys ever have a serious argument?" He turned to Bill Hackensack again.

"We're always on the same line," the man said.

"Well, there you have it!" said Pappas. "The only way to find out if you have some kind of respect for each other is to have an argument and see if the glue holds. Never trust a guy who always agrees with you!"

There was another break. Commercials rushed through the room. Carl smiled at his guests. Dad Hackensack looked a little bit pissed off, so it seemed. The son showed not a trace of any feeling on his face. The other father and son, the Afficionades, both smiled mildly. When the short break was over, without a word at the radio table being spoken, Pappas resumed.

"I'm not sure I like what I'm hearing. You Hackensack people seem to be worried about the business and the money more than you are concerned about people. How's that for you, Moon? You're on the board of Afficionades Media already, your father is the chairman, how do you two get along?"

"We fight all the time," said Moon.

"Not all the time," protested his father.

"Oh come on dad. We're doing it now!"

"What do you guys argue about then?" Carl asked.

For a while father and son Hackensack talked simultaneously. The bizz jockey interrupted them and then allowed Moon to answer the question first.

"My father wants me to take over the business when he

retires. That will be a long time from now, because he's really, like, young. I'm just not sure if I want to wait till I'm in my fifties before I'm in charge. What if I want to do a business of my own right now and not in, like, thirty years? I like being on the board and stuff, but that's not the point."

"Why go around doing start-ups when you can be one of the owners of a conglomerate like Afficionades Media?" yelled Rog.

"So I can make some decisions of my own instead of having to argue with you all the time," said Moon.

"Nevertheless you guys have been working together for a couple of years now," said the bizz jockey. "You're not really going anywhere without your father's consent, it seems."

"In the media business my father's the best," said Moon. "I can learn more from him than from anyone else."

"Is it me or is the air in this room getting sticky with slime?" barked Carl Pappas right into the microphone. "I know you people have business interests to protect. I know that if there's too much disagreement between you there'll be ripples on Wall Street and in Hong Kong and everywhere else. But you are also role models who need to be honest about things. There's nothing you can hide on The Boardroom, because the whole world will know you guys are puttin' on a show."

"We're not putting on a show, Mr. Pappas," said Rog, looking to the other men at the table. They all nodded in approval.

"You are not going to get away with this old school attitude," said Carl, who sounded really angry now.

Beyond the window, Hitomi frowned. She didn't like the

sound of the bizz jockey's voice. She was an expert in detecting real, genuine Carl Pappas anger from a fake. The difference eluded most people. Even Don Wozniak, who was supposed to have an ear for everything.

"If you don't have some kind of opinion about your father or your son, as a person, if you only have a eye for the business side of things, then how can you people be believable CEOs for the thousands of people who work for you?"

"We call it being professional, Carl," said Bill.

"Professional my ass. People want to know if you actually give a damn about people. If you don't care about how your son really feels then how are we to believe you care about the environment? About the glass ceiling for women? About the working class? About anything?"

Rog Afficionades hesitated before he responded. "You got a point there, Carl. But how is one to really know? I mean, I hate to admit it, but ultimately there is no way of really knowing how my children feel about me."

"Of course you can. You can put them to the test. That is... if you really want to know. But I'm starting to think you people actually don't care at all."

"But I do," said Rog.

The other men at the table all agreed.

"Yes! I do too!"

"Course we care!"

"What's this test then, Carl?"

Hitomi looked nervously into her papers; a stack of sheets clipped together on a board that contained all the topics of the night's show, including all the one-liners and off-hand remarks that were written by Job Messner. There was no mention of any test. She was already worried by Carl's angry voice, but now she was feeling something worse. It could be nausea.

"I'm not just talking to you guys here," said Pappas. "I'm talking to all you rich folks listening. If you got kids, how do you know they like you? With kids it's the same thing as with friends: if you're famous or rich, odds are that they're faking it. You can't be Tom Cruise and expect to make new friends. People like you because of your fame and wealth. I know a lot of you folks can live with that. But if you can't, if you are coming from a cold place and are moving into a more Buddhist approach here — I'm not saying I'm a Buddhist, just for the record — you need to find out who's honest. Who are your real friends? And what's more: do your kids love you or do they merely tolerate you? The only way to find this out, people, is to give all your money away."

Oh my, thought Hitomi. He's lost it. That was the stupidest joke since Carl had told Richard Branson to not just fly around the planet but to stay in orbit. If it was a joke. Tell me it's a joke, she thought. Please? Please, please me Carl Pappas.

There was some protest coming from the table.

"The only proof of friendship from your kids is that they still love you if they get no money at all. Isn't that so? Here's what you get: you either find out they still love you, which is OK because you can't take money with you to the grave. Or you find out they actually hate you and at least you've unmasked them."

"This is such nonsense," said William Hackensack the

third. "Blah blah. You can't take money to the grave, but you sure as hell can't take any love either! Why give away all that money when..."

"When what?" said his father. "Well? I'm actually starting to get curious here. I mean, this is all purely theoretical, of course, but ain't that also kinda innarestin'? How would you feel if I gave it all away?"

"Mother would never, never let you."

At this point all the men in the room started meddling with the discussion, except for the bizz jockey, who sat back and smiled. At last something was underway. Beyond the room, in the viewing chamber, the guests' entourage could be seen in an uproar; all of a sudden everybody was talking.

A look was exchanged between the bizz jockey and his producer. One looked content. The other looked unnerved.

Six

By the time Carl Pappas reached the roof of the parking garage the night was well on the way. He had been in a row with the WCBN Radio boss Phil Solo about the way he had been handling today's The Boardroom. It's not really worth mentioning as these rows were almost standard procedure, but tonight had been an exceptionally tedious discussion. In the end Carl had simply left Solo's office, stating that the boss obviously had too many rich friends and was now worried about his network falling apart in the aftermath of the show. True, it had been a strong program today, with lots of challenges and some serious callers insulting both the host and his guests.

On the whole, though, it was successful once again. That's how Carl felt. At least one of his guests had decided to go along with the bizz jockey and respond to the issue of rich parents vs. rich kids, thus creating some tension while the show was live. He had no real idea about the impact of the show on the outside world yet, because Carl never hung around very long after the show. Usually he withdrew quickly because talking for a whole hour on the peak of his ability always exhausted him.

Close to his car stood Hitomi. She was leaning against a huge four-wheel drive, vaguely lit by a lamp from above. But not quite vaguely enough, because the bizz jockey clearly saw that she was talking to Moon Afficionades, the guy in the camouflage suit, his slick hair combed backwards, only his sunglasses gone for the night. They were standing too close for comfort.

So just to be on the safe side Carl coughed and they looked at him, startled.

"Don't you guys ever watch crime series?" said Carl. "The ones with the creepy serial killers who stalk their victims on parking garage roofs?"

"We were just talking about the show," said Hitomi, who appeared to be a little bit nervous, so very unlike her usual self. "Moon's really upset about some of the things you said."

"Is he now?"

Moon Afficionades was wearing an army parka over his camouflage suit. He stretched his hand and touched Pappas' shoulder. "You've stirred things up quite a bit," he said. "What if some billionaire decides to take your crazy ideas seriously and give all his money away and test his children?"

"You have nothing to worry about," said Carl. "Your father didn't strike me as that kind of a man."

The young man tightened his grip on Carl's shoulder. "I wouldn't bet my life on that," he said. "But if he turns out to be just that kind of a man, I'll come looking for you, buddy."

"Are you... threatening me, Afficionades? Or are we about to become friends?"

Right before it started to hurt, Moon let go of the bizz

jockey's shoulder. The two men looked each other in the eye for a moment. Then, from the shades, two men in dark suits wearing sunglasses emerged from the shadows of the entrance, where the elevator was.

This was all too embarrassing for Hitomi, who snapped out of her unusual lethargy and slapped both men on the back. She was an athletic woman and the slap had an audible impact.

"Jeez Sakamoto…" howled Carl.

"Guys. We had a fun evening. It was a success. This girl is going to ask for a raise. The BJ is getting more listeners. And you, Moon, you will get credit for speaking candidly on live radio."

The men shook hands. Then they all stood there, watched by the security guys a few meters away.

"Well, if nobody needs a ride I'm outta here," said Carl. He turned, walked to his car, got in and started the engine without looking back. He drove right by the whole group, so he could envelope them in the thick blue cloud of the exhaust fumes his old timer produced. In the rear mirror he saw the two security guys looking back, while Hitomi and Moon stepped into some other car.

The bizz jockey felt odd. Someone had stepped forward and blocked his direct line with his producer.

Should I be concerned about her safety? he thought. I guess not. The Afficionades live in the limelight, they are responsible people with bodyguards. I could text her tomorrow just to check on her.

She'll be back on Monday, he thought as his car dived on the ramp downwards.

Seven

The next morning even before opening his eyes Carl stretched out a hand to touch either his girlfriend or a vacant lot in his king-sized bed. Obviously she had already left for work. Nothing out of the ordinary so far, but the bizz jockey didn't like it nevertheless. She hadn't been home last night when he returned. That wasn't anything out of the ordinary either, but he hadn't liked it nevertheless. What was an attractive young woman, with legs as long as you can get them, smelling like a rose garden, with hair like a black fountain and a smile that made a man forget himself, what was such a woman doing in the city beyond midnight? Carl had always laughed at other men's infidelities because of her. But last night's broadcast had annoyed him and brought him slightly off balance.

The only remedy for this would be a cold shower along with some serious coffee. So he took his cup of coffee along with him and stepped into the shower booth, right under the cold stream. That didn't necessarily work out well.

Ten minutes later Carl sat in the kitchen, a plaster on his toe that he had administered after stepping into a shard of his coffee mug that had fallen onto the bathroom floor as a result of the cold-water shock that had come over him.

"Don't do that again," he muttered, sipping from the second mug filled with new coffee. He held the mug carefully on the table and contemplated the medical side of a flesh wound on the toe. Had he cleaned it well enough?

He switched on the TV and let the rush of CNN come over him. The host of the news show, the super model type, looked like she was talking about Gucci's latest collection, when in reality the item at hand was an apparent landslide in South America that had cost thousands of lives.

Carl picked up his mobile phone and called Hitomi.

"Carl Evangelos Pappas, it's way too early for you to be calling, so whatever's wrong, let's hear it right away because I'm in the middle of something," his producer rattled away before he could say anything.

"Just get on CNN and check that super model talking about death again," said Carl. "We really need to get them to the show so I can grill them someday. Have you been working on that?"

"All the girls at CNN and Al Jazeera and CCTV and the BBC know how you feel about them, Carl, you've voiced that so often that they plan to stay clear of The Boardroom for quite a while yet, no thanks."

"No thanks. Listen, I'm a little worried about you and that billionaire's son, Io or Jupiter or what's his name," said Carl.

"You know his name very well, Carl Evangelos Pappas," said Hitomi with the tone that had made her powerful in the business, because it was the kind of tone that may either suggest anger or be just that. No way of knowing.

Then there was a silence.

"Don't tell me he's with you right now, Sakamoto," said Carl, gasping for air.

"You need to discuss stuff? Otherwise I need to call you back in an hour."

"No. I need you to come to the Gulag in an hour. We need to go through some of the topics we came up with. Just you and me."

"Will Philemon Solo be there too?"

"No to my knowledge he ain't. What do you think, I'm going to sit there and listen to the two of you argue and shout?"

"How about me going all the way over to the Gulag and listen to the two of you agree on everything?"

Of course nobody ever agreed on anything with Phil Solo.

"I have to be completely candid on this," said Hitomi.

They were sitting in the Gulag exactly one hour later. In front of them, on the table by a window looking out at the sunny morning city, the high-rise buildings of the business district and the river, were Hitomi's tablet and a green broccoli juice. There was also Carl's "black juice", as waitress Katie had said as she brought the stuff over. Whatever was in his cup was almost too black for coffee. It had probably been roasting on the hot plate all morning. After the first sip Carl felt like he had kissed a coal miner. He took a sachet and poured the powdered milk into the coffee.

"A lot of people are really annoyed with last night's topic," Hitomi rattled. "It's more than obvious that you're not a fan of amassed wealth within families and kids who grow up knowing they're basically richer and more powerful than anyone they meet. Not everyone can be rich and be Bono at the same time, you know."

Carl interrupted the Japanese accented stream. "You mean Moon Afficionades is annoyed and he told you so in person. Was that before or after you guys kissed?"

Never one to be easily impressed, Hitomi answered: "While we were working out." She sipped her juice.

Carl looked on in disgust at the green stuff at her upper lip, and speechless at her reply. What he was thinking was this: Should I ask her about the exact details of "working out"? He decided not to.

"Yes, Moon is also not amused. It was actually quite scary, he got into a rant last night when we... I had to snap him out of it."

Carl looked her straight in the eye. Hitomi didn't blink. Then Carl burst into a big smile, a silent laugh.

"You want to know how I snapped him out of his rant," said Hitomi in that unique Japanese style, a sentence without melody.

A touch of Arnold Schwarzenegger's accent in there as well, thought Carl. He looked out the window. Last thing he wanted to get into was the physical aspect of Hitomi Sakamoto's private life. Even in her early forties she had an athlete's body as a result of endless park jogging and gym sessions. She had more energy than Carl himself, and that was saying something. The bizz jockey always considered himself a loyal friend to his girl, but he had also learned to keep a safe distance from attractive women. Especially women he worked with. So he gazed across the river for a moment and then looked at Hitomi again.

"Exactly what did he say?" he asked.

"He sort of repeated what he said on the parking roof. If his father ever gets any funny ideas about giving away his billions, Moon will come knocking on your door."

"That is downright stupid. Is he stupid? It was philosophical. It was just a joke to get these refrigerators to respond to what I was talking about. They weren't talking, so I got them to talk. The phone started ringing. That's what it's all about, isn't it?"

The waitress appeared.

"Katharina Yekaterina," said Hitomi. "I'd like another broccoli juice. And he'll have more of that black stuff. Very un-Tao, but there you are."

"Yes ma'am," said Katie and walked off.

"And I still believe that calling a restaurant 'Gulag' is offensive to a great many people still alive today!' growled Hitomi after her. Then she said to Carl: "I believe he was genuinely offended. He also got several calls from other brats and some of them were even more offended. One of them wanted to come over and pay you a visit."

"And send his bodyguards in first, no doubt," said Carl. "And when was he taking all these calls, Hitomi. At breakfast?"

"Don't you give me no crap about doin' some billionaire's kid for his money, Carl Evangelos Pappas."

"At least you admit," grinned the bizz jockey. "Listen, I don't doubt your choices of men for a second. You're too clever to make mistakes. Enjoy the dude. I'm drinking my coffee, how about you reading me the agenda?"

"How about that indeed."

Eight

"Carl, is your car parked outside?" said Katie, almost at the end of their morning meeting, when they were about to wrap it up.

"Yes it is," said Carl. "But let's keep that amongst ourselves."

For any bystander that would have been a poor attempt at a joke, but the insiders recognized it as one of the bizz jockey's running gags. Not particularly funny in itself, but amusing for its repetitiveness through the years.

"You better go check it out," said the waitress, unmoved. "I think it's burning."

"What the f...," Carl started, looking out the window, seeing nothing as the parking lot was around the corner, at the north end of the Gulag café. "Don't try to be funny at the expense of my loyal old timer."

"Don't worry about it. We called the fire department a couple of minutes ago, but it only just now occurred to me it might be your car."

The bizz jockey and the Russian waitress looked each other deep in the eye and remained locked like that for a moment.

Hitomi Sakamoto snapped Carl out of it by saying: "That's not funny enough to be a joke!"

Exactly at that time they heard a siren coming from outside, from a distance, approaching really fast. Then it suddenly was very close, there was a roaring engine and then... silence again.

"The cook saw it first," said Katie, sort of apologetic towards Carl and Hitomi, who had gotten up in a hurry and were rushing out the door.

They took two right turns and walked onto the parking lot. There was a fire truck standing alongside and a couple of firemen looking at the tires. The car looked all right but all four tires had burned and melted. The stench was exactly what you might expect.

"Excuse me, that's my car... What the... Jesus!" Carl cursed.

"Looks like you were lucky, sir," said one of the firemen.

"Lucky? And why is that?"

"It's just the tires, sir. All four of them melted away."

"Isn't that a bit unusual?" said Hitomi.

"You can call it extraordinary!" said the fireman. "And twice!"

"Twice?"

"The tires burned but the rest of your car didn't catch fire," said the fireman. "That's also extraordinary."

A police car arrived, two officers got out.

"Ah, Mr. Pappas," said one officer. "That your car?"

"Do I know you?"

"No. And you don't have to. We know you."

"We want to report arson," said Hitomi. "At the very least. But it looks like an assassination attempt, to be sure."

"Oh come on, Hitomi. That is not an assassination attempt, that's ridiculous!" said Carl. "It's a prank!"

"No way," said the fireman. "Four wheels burning at the same time, that's not a prank, that's a message."

"Again, officer, we want to file both arson and... Oh... Hi, Moon," said Hitomi.

Moon Afficionades walked towards them. Carl had no idea where the guy came from. His sunglasses were back prominently, hovering over the camouflage suit.

"What's going on here?" said Moon and then he embraced Hitomi and they kissed.

After that, Hitomi gave Carl a look, but he wasn't sure if it meant "don't you dare comment" — which was what it looked like.

"Someone did something to my old timer," said Carl. "It doesn't look like a coincidence."

"For the life of me, I don't understand why you don't have a bodyguard," said Moon. "You provoke so many people, unleash so much anger, I should worry about my safety if I were you. Today it's your car... tomorrow it's your shoes."

"Very funny, Afficionades," said Carl. "Are you by any chance one of these provoked people? Any particular anger I have unleashed?"

Moon's face darkened, even though he tried not to show it. "Actually I am and you have," he said. "But that's my problem, isn't it?"

They stood very close now.

Then Carl turned to the police officer and said: "I do want to report this, officer. Four wheels burning, that's someone giving me a message."

"You're pissing off ten million people on a daily basis, Mr. Pappas," laughed the officer.

"I am not pissing off ten million people, officer. I have ten million LISTENERS. There's a huge difference!"

"Of course it's always good to report it. It looks very suspicious, not like an ordinary act of vandalism."

"I'll drive you to the station," said Hitomi.

"You can go with him," said Carl grim. "I can handle my hate mail, thank you."

"No way," said Hitomi, her voice emphasizing that debating her decision was useless. "Otherwise I'll have to answer to Philemon Solo for abandoning you and I'd rather not do that." Then, to Moon: "We'll reschedule."

Then she grabbed her mobile phone and started calling a recovery service.

Moon smiled at Carl.

"So you're not here by coincidence," said Carl. "That's good."

"You mean good as in: a good alibi?" said Moon.

"Those are your words, buddy."

Moon made one last remark before he left. "I still think you should consider this arson as a message to you, Mr. Bizz Jockey." Then he walked off.

"I agree," said the police officer. "Well, we'll see you downtown for your report then?"

"You can count on that," said Carl. He looked at his car, saddened. "Whoever did this has no respect for vintage cars."

"Lack of respect, a sign of the times," said the police officer.

Nine

So what if this billionaire's kid is behaving like an angry young man, Carl thought. He was sitting in his office on the seventeenth floor of the WCBN building, looking at the city as darkness settled over it. It was the first time that day that he had found the peace to think things over. So the first thing he did was dismiss the idea of Moon Afficonades having set his car on fire. The thought itself was ridiculous. There was no reason for the new generation of wealthy business people to be alarmed by anything that happened on The Boardroom.

We had a funny talk about love versus money, Pappas thought, and I made a joke about giving it all away in order to test the genuine family ties. Family ties should not be all about money, should they?

The thing that really worried him, though, was his producer's behavior. She was channeling the wrong kind of emotions to him. She had always been frank about the work and her views, but it was never personal. There was never anything disturbing about the information she provided; it was all for the benefit of the world's best business talk radio.

And now she gave him this bullshit about the rich kids

being pissed off.

He looked at the city. At the lights shimmering in the diminishing heat of the past day. It was a night for an evening dinner and a glass of wine with his beautiful woman. That was a luxury he could only afford on Saturday and Sunday nights. So his beautiful woman would probably be in some roof garden, with a glass of wine and some company.

It's a tough life being a bizz jockey sometimes.

"I don't need that shit from you," was the first thing he hissed when he and Hitomi met in the studio a while later.

No one was around yet, not even sound engineer Don Wozniak.

"Excuse me?"

"Stop horsing me around with your new lover's opinions about me," said Carl. "He's mistaking me for someone who gives a shit."

"Don't lie to me, Carl Evangelos Pappas," said Hitomi firmly. "You don't seem to be taking it lightly."

"OK. So you win. You happy now? All this innuendo is getting to me and I can't explain it. Whatever's going on with you and this man from the moon... You are saying or he is saying that some of these kids are mad enough to hit me in the face or worse. I don't need that. I need to concentrate on the show. Dammit Hitomi, you're supposed to keep these people away from me, not channel them directly to me."

There was a silence.

Then there were filthy noises coming from someone's throat in the hall outside the studio.

Hitomi rolled here eyes with unusual intensity.

There were lights flickering on in the sound room on the other side of one of the internal studio windows and the voice of Don Wozniak came through the sound system: "Oh. Hi you guys. What's up?"

"I'm sorry," whispered Hitomi in Carl's ear, outside of Don's earshot. "You're right. I'll take care of it. You don't seriously believe Moon set your car on fire, I asked him to come there and..."

"You're doing it again, Hitomi!"

They both smiled.

Exactly at that moment Don walked in, clearing his throat again.

Because he's a filthy bugger, thought Hitomi.

Because he wants us to know he's walking into the room, thought Carl.

When the show kicked off, Carl Pappas was still irritated by all this. But being the professional that he was, he pushed aside his feelings and got into the hang of it, into the hang of live radio, while the WCBN voice hammered out the opening lines. Right before it was over and it was his turn, his crispy thinking returned, undisturbed by anything he didn't want to be disturbed by.

"...This is The Boardroom. Here is your prophet, the buddy and the bodyguard of every CEO, the Don Juan of every business babe. Here is the world's one and only bizz jockey. Here is your BJ: Carl Pappas!"

"Men and women of the business, welcome to The Boardroom," he said, very slowly, with much emphasis on the seventh word. "Where just like any other day we ask ourselves: where do we stand? If you know the answer, you may call now. But don't take this lightly; many went before you. Many were mistaken. And are grounded now, in court, in jail or in hell. A few moments from now I will be talking to the CEO of the largest Japanese-Chinese merger today, and I guess you people all know who I'm talking about. They'll be talking live from their seats in Tokyo and Beijing, though it may be that you'll be hearing an interpreter's voice for the Chines guy, I'm not sure. But before we get into that, did I tell you about the two CEO's sitting in a business lounge on some airport. 'My son's got a position on the board but he hardly ever shows up. He's at the tennis court most of the time,' says one CEO. So the other guy, you know, he's learned that positive feedback brings you further into this world, so he says: 'Is he any good at it?' And of course, this works. The first CEO says: 'No. He's terrible. Once he lost a big match and then he bought the whole club and had the place torn down and put condo's there. Then he sold it for a huge profit and used the money to build TWO whole new tennis clubs where he could hang out even longer.' Now the morale of this story, people, is that if you got a kid who's just hangin' around playing and chasing girls, they may stumble upon their true talent somewhere along the way."

Don Wozniak nodded in Carl's direction, they exchanged a look and then the sound engineer started a short jingle, something like "W.W.W. Cee Bee NNN!"

Then it was time for the usual round of incoming phone calls. People could get through to a switchboard somewhere else in the building, from all over the world, a selection of whom were transferred to Don Wozniak. Many calls came from countries where it was the middle of the night, made by business people who got up at some odd hour just to be on the show. Actually calls kept coming in 24 hours a day because there was always some radio station broadcasting the show somewhere in the world, and the actual live air time of the show was not always clear to its listeners. At the end of the line, after approval by Hitomi, some of them were transferred to Carl's earphones, along with a small description of the caller's name and topic on the laptop screen in front of him.

"This is Carl Pappas. You may speak."

"Hello Carl, this is Stephen. I want to thank you for yesterday's show, that was really inspiring."

"Much obliged, Stephen. Now I don't want to be a nuisance but you do realize that our readers are not interested in friendly chit chat? If that'll be all I'm gonna hang you up right..."

"Got something for you there, Carl. I'm going to do it. There. I said it."

"Do what, Stephen?"

"Test my children's loyalty to me and their mother by giving all our money away."

The bizz jockey's mouth fell open as he looked straight at Hitomi. Am I looking for support here, he thought, or am I blaming her?

But a sudden jerk of Hitomi's head put him back to the show right away.

"OK Stephen, stay calm. I'm going to repeat what you just said," Carl said.

He made a gesture to Don while he said that, and the sound

engineer replayed the entire sentence on his console with one hand, as if it was nothing. As if it required no skills whatsoever.

"Test my children's loyalty to me and their mother by giving all our money away."

"Now why on earth would you want to do that?" said Carl. He sounded uptight, as if the whole topic was bringing him off balance. "What did your kids do to you or your wife that makes you want to punish them?"

"Well, it was your idea, Mr. Bizz Jockey."

"What business are you in Stephen? Have you been successful?"

"I'm in prophylactics and yes, I've been successful."

"Not by doing what you were told, I suppose?"

"No. I followed my own plan."

"Then why start following someone else's orders now? What's your plan this time, Stephen?"

"Money corrupts people," said the man on the phone. There was a slight static disturbance on the line, but he was still audible. "I've seen many old friendships go down the drain once I got really rich. In friendships it's easier to detect that kind of behavior. But with kids it's difficult. My wife and I have decided to follow up on your suggestion and go for the love. I'm tired of having to be sharp all the time, keep the sharks away from my money. As soon as I got nothing anymore, we'll know who really likes us and who doesn't. Without knowing it, I've longed for that for years."

"There's also a lot of sharks around when you're poor, Stephen," sighed Carl.

"You know what I'm talking about, Carl," said Stephen. "It's a spiritual thing. That's your gift, I suppose. You should be happy for me."

For a moment Carl wondered if he should say that he had simply been joking. That giving all your money away to test your kids was a joke. But he was not so sure anymore. Perhaps it had been a joke, but it had certainly not been an attempt at being spiritual, or at least Pappas didn't think so. Could that be the case? Could it be that some of his listeners thought of the Bizz Jockey as a spiritual guide? He'd have to check with Hitomi and Phil, because he didn't like the idea. He did not like that at all. Of course there was always a bit of bantering about the deeper psyche of the business man and woman. The meaning of life and that sort of stuff popped up every now and then, because after many years of hard labor many people either backed away from corporate life because they were ready to retire in the sun or because they simply collapsed, and in both cases they were confronted with that pivotal question: what has all that work done for me? But those were also the people who stopped listening to The Boardroom because they no longer cared deeply about business. Their thoughts were drifting elsewhere. The bulk of Carl's audience was not interested in the meaning of life; they were interested in doing business and doing it good. And looking good doing it.

Ten

"Are you nuts?" asked Carl.

He was talking to Neil Kalen on his cell phone. Kalen was his buddy of many years, an old hippie millionaire who happened to have had one huge worldwide number one hit single on the charts a long time ago, a nice little song that could be heard on radios all over the world for at least two decades now and that still paid off huge amounts of money every year. Neil was still searching for his next success song after all these years, but every album he had recorded had tanked. In spite of his ongoing search for a new song the lack of success didn't seem to bother him. He was always composing, performing, painting and hanging out with old groupies, women that had matured but remained girls the way some women remain girls because of how they wear their hair and the way they dress and, most of all, because of the energy they still have. Neil Kalen was a man who never worried and that was probably, in Carl's opinion, the biggest reason for his failure to come up with a new song. Carl thought of the successful artist as someone who had to be tormented in some way. Happiness works for Paul McCartney only.

"Of course I'm nuts," said Neil. "What the hell kinda question is that?"

"I mean because you're rich. Does all that money do something to you, put you outside of reality?"

"Carl you're making no sense at all. I... Wait... Of course darling, of course Linda can come over too... Yeah sure... Carl, what are you asking, really?"

"People who have to work most of their lives are in touch with reality because, well, they are not in a position to say 'no' to other people. You need to be amicable with your boss, your neighbors, your family, your spouse and so on. If you're rich you can piss everybody off and they'll still kiss your boots because your rich. That's what I mean. Is that so? Can you confirm that?"

"Jesus Carl. The stuff you come up with."

"Just answer me, Neil."

"OK," Neil sighed.

In the background there was a woman laughing. Carl smiled. I have to get together with Neil one of these days, he thought. Sit back and relax for a moment, inhale some of his craziness.

Neil carried on: "Money creates a distance between myself and everybody else, except for the people I've known before I became rich and famous. It's as simple as that. And you're right, I can pretty much do as I please. Even if I ended up in jail, I'd still be getting shitloads of money. You happy now? You happy now that you've reduced all human relationships to money?"

"Not all people's relationships, Neil. Just those of you rich guys."

Then Carl explained to Neil how some rich entrepreneur was going to give all his money away to test his kids, just because the Bizz Jockey told him to.

"Wow. That's cool, man. That's awesome. These kids... They're going to kill him!"

"You think so? No, skip that. I didn't ask that."

"Separate a dude from his money, that's the worst thing you can do to anyone. Or they'd have to become a Buddhist or something. So you suggested this, Carl, huh?"

"It was like a joke."

"No it wasn't. You're not that kind of a joker. There's a preacher inside you, Carl. When are going to admit that?"

"I'll buy you dinner next week. We need to catch up, old man. Just as long as you don't start this preacher shit with me."

"Forget about next week. See you at eight, the usual place."

They hung up. They always hung up this way. No delays, no show.

Carl was sitting with nothing in his head, because a dinner date with Neil always made him feel good. He liked a man who didn't change. Here was an old hippie that was still a hippie, still free, still believing what he believed thirty years ago. A man who had not been lured into the business side of music. He would just play a gig now and then, here and there, and perhaps release an album on his own, waiting for the big song to come along. Neil always cheered him up, so he was contemplating this old friendship when the porter rang from downstairs. There followed some blah blah — apparently his rental car, replacing his old timer till it was repaired, was being delivered downstairs on the orders of Hitomi. So he took the elevator downstairs to the lobby of his apartment building and talked to the porter.

"The guy drove down into the garage," said the porter. "I opened the doors for him so you don't have to do any parking and you don't have to go out, it's a stormy night. He's in the D section, waiting for you."

"That's way more service than I've had in years," said Carl, smiling to the porter. He walked away from the desk, went through a door and took the stairs down to the garage beneath the apartment complex.

The D section was the lowest level of the parking garage. There was plenty of space here, as the building had been constructed in the long gone era of plenty, and few building occupants ever got that far down. In all these years as an apartment owner Carl had been here maybe once, maybe twice, maybe never. It was also a part of the building that was in stark contrast with the clean, white, freshly painted facade: many of the old fluorescent lamps were broken and there was the moist smell of fungus. There were lots of shadows and as expected there were zero cars. It occurred to Carl that as an apartment owner he was also paying for this unused mess, this rotting bottom under his castle.

Then he heard an engine start and a car appeared from the shadows. It drove a little bit too swiftly towards him, its tires squeaking. Then it came to a halt right in front of him. Carl walked over to the driver's seat, and the initial feeling of being honorably serviced evaporated when he looked right through the open driver's window, into the barrel of a gun.

Eleven

Don Wozniak got the shock of a lifetime. Or one of those shocks, because it was not the first time that Neil Kalen walked into his engineer's booth and he just never got used to seeing the big man. When Don had been a boy, which in many ways he still was as far as Hitomi Sakamoto was concerned, he had been a huge fan of Kalen's one hit wonder, that one time summer hit song that had blocked the number one slot of the worldwide hit parades for months. For thirty weeks in a row the Billboard Hot One Hundred had been topped by Kalen's composition, an upbeat dance song that was loved by crowds in dance halls and at beach barbecues and wherever young people went for a good time. So to Don, Neil Kalen was an übermensch, a super hero, even if that one song was all he had ever brought to the airwaves.

"N-Neil," he stammered, "man…"

"Dude," said Neil, "I seem to have forgotten your name again. I hope you're not embarrassed by this, it looks like its turning into a running gag but it's because I've something else on my mind. You got a moment for me?"

"Loads of moments," said Don. "And it's Don."

"Are you related to Don Henley by any chance?" said Neil.

The sound engineer looked puzzled.

"The Eagles' singer and drummer. You know, he sings 'Hotel California'?" said Neil. "Oh well, never mind. Hey, you know that song by any chance, 'Oh Well'? Listen, I was supposed to meet Carl for dinner but he never showed up. His girlfriend's out of the country — what's new — and he's not answering his cell phone."

"Tried his apartment?" said Don. "He could be on the couch with a hangover. It's Friday night, right?"

Neil suddenly and violently grabbed Don by his shirt and pulled him close. There was the breath of whiskey and nicotine.

"For Carl Pappas the show goes on always," he said. "And I mean always. You've worked with him for a century. Has there ever been a no-show with Carl?"

"Never," sounded the firm voice of Hitomi from the door.

They both looked at her. Neil let go of Don's shirt.

Don backed off.

"He must have had an accident, there can't be any other explanation," said Hitomi as she drew her cell phone and started dialing.

Neil paced the room nervously as Hitomi talked to her liaison at the police station and then to the desk at Carl's apartment building, while Don watched him closely, repositioning his T-shirt.

After she had terminated the short conversation, Hitomi addressed the men again. "No news from the police. The porter at his place says Carl went down into the garage to get his new rental car and that's the last he saw of him, about three hours ago."

Then she dialed another number.

"Who're you calling this time, girl?" said Neil.

"Probably her new billionaire boyfriend," said Don.

Hitomi shot him a look as if she were about to initiate the next ice age. They all heard a voicemail beep coming from her phone. She hung up without leaving a message.

"Everybody runs," she said, "and I'm stuck here with you useless people."

Don looked pissed, but Neil smiled.

"Perhaps we should alert Phil Solo," Don tried.

"He'd just laugh," said Hitomi. "What are you going to say: 'your bizz jockey has been kidnapped'?"

"You said yourself that Carl always shows up," said Don. "What's the big deal here anyway? What if he has a flat tire? What if he's held up for speeding? What if he ran into a traffic jam?"

"I dunno, dude," said Neil Kalen. "Carl knows I'm waiting for him. He's never late. He never lets anybody wait. So I wait for a whole hour. He never calls my cell phone. He doesn't answer his own. Something's up. I'm going to report him missing. Listen, miss Japanese producer, I'd appreciate it if you came along, you seem to have the right amount of authority for the police."

"All right," said Hitomi. "We need to take this seriously. Don Lech Wozniak, if Carl's girlfriend happens to call, try not to alarm her by asking stupid questions. Can you do that?"

"Any stupid questions in particular?"

"Yeah, that's stupid enough."

===

Outside, under the night sky, an unconscious man was dragged out of a car and carried across a boardwalk towards a speedboat that was slamming up and down on the choppy waters of the river, like a staggering thoroughbred. On the other side, the office buildings of the business district were relaxing at the start of the weekend, many of their windows still brightly lit for the convenience of the cleaning personnel doing their appointed rounds. They were vacuuming with their headphones on, listening to their favorite muzak and oblivious to the stormy weather outside and the fate of the world's number one bizz jockey.

Twelve

Regrets came seldom to Carl Pappas. He was not the type for it. A couple of times a year he went too far insulting his audience, depending on your point of view of course. But no matter how heavy public opinion came down on WCBN Radio, no matter how angry the managing director became over the lawsuits and the threats and the lawyers' bills, Carl always justified himself by saying that it was all in a knight's stride. Yes, he was famous for his uncanny ability to attack like a warrior without even a moment's notice, and to sound like a crusader against the worldwide capital, against the establishment — even if he was really on their side too. He felt that his ability to strike first was one of the reasons his radio show The Boardroom was so successful to begin with and therefore regretting any of his outbursts was basically counterproductive.

He did not think that now.

At first, when he woke up slowly, he thought nothing and just felt the painful upper arm where he had been injected after being forced to mount the car. He concluded that his body seemed to be functioning properly, so he opened his eyes and tested his visual and hearing and thinking functions simultaneously.

Carl saw a primitive bedroom around him, obviously part of some outdoor hut. The window was closed by a shutter on the outside. Besides the bed, one chair and a standing lamp the room was empty. Outside there were no city noises; there was the sound of a soft wind. Or could that be waves in the distance?

Pappas thought: my big mouth has gotten me in trouble.

Then he remembered what the man in the car had said before injecting him.

"You are going to take back what you said, Mr. Radio Dick."

Carl thought back to the only time in his career when he had lost his courage, when he had struck that particular raw nerve of the worldwide business community: oil. This had happened years ago and as he had been contemplating a possible retreat, his boss Phil Solo had stood up and said loudly: "No one shuts up the bizz jockey!"

And had walked to the door of his office, and shouted through the corridor, for all staff to hear: "No one shuts up the bizz jockey. You hear me?"

Carl felt a smile come up, but it didn't make it to his lips. This was no time to be cherishing memories, this was a time for grim realism. He felt his pockets and to his surprise everything was still there. All the stuff that makes a 21st century man. Keys. Wallet. Cell phone. For a moment he felt lucky, but of course it was only beginner's luck: the phone battery was dead. This could mean his abductors had forgotten to take the phone away from him. If that were the case, how bad could it all be?

On the other hand, being sedated by injection, being abducted and locked in some cabin outside the city was bad enough as it was. It was all right to get one's hopes up, but that was no excuse to get all exited, as Carl soon found out when he tried to walk to the door. Sitting up on the bed and placing his feet on the ground made him all dizzy and he had to lie down again.

Then, as he lay flat on the blanket, the horror of it all struck him. What if he didn't make it back in time for the next broadcast of The Boardroom? What if he'd already missed one?

By the time someone came into the room, hours later, Carl was very angry. He had progressed from initial disinterest to genuine fear and finally developed a total grumpiness, which he'd slumped into trying to figure out who was doing this to him. He had gone through a list of suspects in his head. Terrorists? No, these were existing more or less entirely outside his realm — he had never done a show on the financial side of terrorism, on how these people funded their seventy virgins in heaven. Corporate lunatics trying to shut him up? They were too well aware of his powers; piss off the bizz jockey and you may be standing in the middle of Wall Street in the morning with your pants down. Someone who was ruined because of something he had said on live radio? That was possible, but it also wasn't very likely. It had happened a few times, but the actual demise of some company or CEO was never really caused by the bizz jockey. It was merely exposed or accelerated. The larger audience never really blamed him, and neither did the judges for that matter.

A stalker? Perhaps some corporate clerk, a loyal listener for many years, had suddenly responded to some lingering madness deep inside him. The comfort of the bed and the quiet outside could mean that this stalker wanted his guest, the famous bizz jockey, to feel at home.

Then the door opened and immediately Carl dismissed the stalker option.

"What time is it? I need to go on the air."

He was stared at by billionaire slash entrepreneur Bill Gates and pop singer slash poverty warrior Bono, or rather he was stared at by two masks resembling these iconic figures. Plastic party masks attached to two unknown bodies. They could only be judged by their clothes and their postures. These bodies were energetic and erect, so they had to be young. Their clothes suggested they were also well off. One of these young men was dressed in a very expensive suit that showed all the marks of this season's fashion as it had been announced a couple of weeks earlier. Twice a year one of the great fashion designers attended The Boardroom to update the business audience, so Carl knew his fashion when he saw it.

"You will go on the air again after you've fixed the mess you created, Mr. Radio Dick," said the guy on the left, the Bill Gates one.

The one wearing the Bono mask was pointing a gun at Carl, twitching it angrily when his target sat up.

"Listen boys, you were probably drunk last night," said Carl. "Happens to the best of us. Now that you mention it, I remember being with Bono and Bill once and Bono got totally pissed and made a spectacle and the next day he had to apologize to Bill, who was a real sport and wouldn't hear nothing of the sort. If you guys walk away right now and leave the door open so I can go home and get on with my show, we'll just forget the whole thing and keep your fathers out of..."

"SHUT UP!" shouted the Bono mask, raising the gun and putting the second hand round it. "All this talking that you do, has anyone ever said that you talk too much? Yakkety yak. On and on you go, I can't stand this! You have to shut the fuck up, mister Radio Dick. Don't you get it? There's no audience for you here."

"Well, you're doing just f..."

At "f" the Bono guy hit Carl with the gun on the side of his head, right above his ear."

"You got a hearing problem, Radio Dick!"

"OK. OK," said the Bill Gates mask. He grabbed the other guy's arm and pulled him backwards gently, until he had sort of parked them at the door again, away from the bed. Then he turned to Carl again. "I'd pipe down a bit, Mr. Pappas. You are here for a reason. We are all into this up to our necks. We are in deep shit and you—" He raised his arm and stretched it and pointed to Carl, "—are going to get us out again."

Carl's head started to throb. He felt blood trickling around his ear. Perhaps this would be a good time to pipe down indeed, to hear what this was all about. "OK," he said. "I was going to say 'hit me', but..." His voice faded. He felt stupid at this attempted pun.

"I told you we need to be tough on him," shouted the Bono mask, approaching again, waving the gun.

Then a blast sounded and a bullet ricocheted in the room

and plopped into the thick wall of wooden planks.

"OK!" yelled Carl. "I'm sorry! I'm listening!"

"Oh. So now you are listening. Well, I'm tired of listening too, so you'll just have to be waiting till I get the energy to talk again. We'll be back. Come on, we're outta here, Jerry."

From behind the Bill Gates mask came a hissing noise, and then a curse. Someone didn't want Carl to know his name was Jerry, but he didn't care, he didn't know any Jerry. It did ring another bell, though.

"When we come back, you better shut up and start listening seriously, asshole. I'm not here for fun, so stop pissing us off. When we get back and you backmouth us again, we'll beat you up real bad."

For a moment they stood there, panting, and then one of them hollered "What the hell!" and before Carl realized what was happening Bono was on top of him, hammering a fist and a gun. The bizz jockey started to grab at his mask, and then the bell rang inside him and woke him up to a thought.

"Moon!" shouted Pappas. "Stop it!"

The guy behind the Bono mask hesitated, the hammering fist and gun stopped in mid-air. Right at that moment the Gates mask grabbed his buddy and dragged him away from Carl. There was no talking, just muffled moans that sounded like a series of curses. It was unclear to Pappas whether one was helping the other stay on his feet, or whether they were fighting. The men retreaded through the door and slammed it shut. Carl could hear how they locked it. He felt his head. Now there was blood around his ear and above his eye, both on the left side.

If that is really Moon I will be able to talk some sense into him, he thought, confident that he had solved some of this mystery, confident in his radio talk show host way. Of course the kid was not wearing his camouflage suit, but as a kidnapper he had probably changed clothes first. That made sense.

Completely out of touch with reality, Hitomi Sakamoto would have said to that.

Thirteen

"Completely out of touch with reality," said Hitomi Sakamoto as she terminated the call on her cell phone. "The police's position on this is that they'll check on Carl's disappearance as soon as a relative has filed a report, and then twenty-four hours after that."

"Carl's girlfriend is out of the country and out of reach," said Phil Solo. "I'm going to use all my relations to find her ASAP." While pronouncing that last word with annoying emphasis he looked around the room. "We got a crisis, people. Luckily there's no Boardroom till Monday which still gives us two days before this gets known." He left the room without waiting for comments or wisecracks or counterarguments.

"Completely out of touch with reality," said Don Wozniak and Hitomi Sakamoto simultaneously, like some background group to a rapper's song, which made Don smile and Hitomi sulk.

"I am not going to wait until the official channels are worked properly," said Hitomi.

"Luigy will kick ass, no doubt," said Don. "That'll get the search going."

"If Carl's in trouble, I would not want to wait for that. It's Saturday, remember? A lot of people switch off their cell phones."

"I don't know anybody who does that, Hitomi."

"You would not. It's the latest thing, Don Lech Wozniak. People these days work on burnout prevention. Haven't you heard? Getting off line on weekends is the first priority, or part of the weekends anyway. It's buzzing all over, all my friends are off line part of the Saturday or Sunday."

"Which part is it going to be, Hitomi, we need to know nów."

"We need to know nothing. We are going to get to work ourselves. First I need to find out where Moon is." She dialed a number.

"Your new boyfriend's missing too?"

Hitomi shrugged.

"He's twenty years younger than you are and about twenty million wealthier. What do you expect? He's probably with some..."

But Hitomi raised a finger while she gave him the foulest look. Then she spoke into the phone. "Moon, it's Hitomi. I need to speak to you and it's urgent. Whapp me or voice me but don't wait. My boss has gone missing, doesn't look good. Keep it to yourself though." Then she pressed the off button again. "We desperately need a lucky break here," she said. "A clue to work with. What if we go sniffing around at Carl's apartment building?"

A man sat on the bench in the afternoon sun with his back to the café, overlooking the river. A cup of cappuccino was on the little table next to him. The wind, softened since last night but still strong enough to blow off his old, sloppy hat. He wanted to get rid of that old hat and purchase something new. A Fedora or something like that. Maybe even a Stetson. But he just never found the time. His nose was battered. His upper lip wore a vertical scar and as a result of this his mustache was incomplete. There was a little bit of dandruff on his dark raincoat and he nervously tapped his right foot. The man was aware of all the stuff that had been turning him into a nervous wreck through the years. At times like these, when there were a few moments to spare as he was waiting, he thought about this. He felt no fear. He felt no anxiety. He felt no rush. Yet he had all the marks of a neurotic man on the run. Perhaps the dangers of his work and his smoking and his late night whiskeys had done this to him. On the other hand, how was an ordinary man who was just trying to get by supposed to compete with all the slick men you saw on TV? The handsome doctors and detectives and adventurers and psycho killers, the smooth men who seemed to be setting the standards in life these days? One was supposed to have whiter teeth at fifty-one than at twenty-one. How about that.

His cell phone vibrated in his coat. He answered it. "Yes?"

A voice said: "The last location of his cell phone is the F-pier at the harbor, two miles from where you are now. It looks like he moved off shore, but the telephone company data doesn't support that."

"Thanks," said the man with the sloppy hat. He pushed the red button on his old cell phone to end the call. Then he got out a small booklet from inside his raincoat, looked up a number and dialed it.

"Hitomi Sakamoto of The Boardroom."

"Miss Sakamoto, you are talking to a friend of Carl Pappas. Do you have a moment?"

"Who are you?"

"A friend will do. Mr. Pappas asked me to look into something and now it seems he has gone missing."

"If you don't tell me who you are right now, mister, I am going to..."

"Relax, ma'am. Just pay attention. I'm a friend. If you don't deal with it, who will? I'm not sure what's going on but it's unlike Carl Pappas to vanish like this. He asked me to check some stuff he was worried about."

"You're a private eye, is that it?" Hitomi started to sound irritated. "There's a private eye hired by Carl," she said to someone else.

"You have to go to the F-pier at the harbor where the luxury speedboats moor," the man said. "That's where the last signal from his cell phone was registered last night."

He pressed the red button again. The conversation was over. He had made the call with a blocked number so the producer of Carl Pappas' show could not call him back. Thus she had no other choice but to go to the pier. Telling her the truth — "I'm Mach One and I'm looking into your new boyfriend's history at Mr. Pappas' request," — was obviously not an option.

Mach One had been called a day earlier by Carl to check up on Moon Afficionades, and that's what he had been doing, and nothing suspicious had come up, and the next morning the bizz jockey was gone. Obviously a cell phone going dead in the middle of the night in the remote harbor of the city was worrisome to begin with. More worrisome were the additional facts: that the phone had not been switched back on by noon, that Carl Pappas did not answer his home phone and that the porter of his apartment complex confirmed that the bizz jockey had not returned. It left Mach One in a bit of a limbo. He didn't want to get involved too much, because he was always to remain the man in the background always, the man whom Carl relied on the get information about anything faster than anybody. People who had disappeared? Unknown contacts behind the curtains in high places? Offshore companies in the tropical shade of some tax haven? A satellite image of some runaway CEO on a swimming pool escarpment? You could count on Ross York, a.k.a. Mach One to most people. There were too many powerful people who had a score to settle with the York character, so it was always best to avoid that name.

It seemed to Mach One that the only favor he could do Carl Pappas right now was to put his producer on his trail. To him, Hitomi Sakamoto was like a secret weapon.

Fourteen

They had moved Carl out of the cabin. His head still hurt, but fortunately the two men had given up beating almost immediately after they'd begun. The walk through a lush garden took long enough for him to take a good look at the environment and do some educated guessing. Obviously they were on a small island. On one side he could see the waters of what could be the Great Lake. There was no sight of the shore. A couple of large speedboats were docked to a wooden pier, across the lawn they were walking on. The rest of the island was covered with bushes and trees, but he could see the shimmering of the sunlight in the lake coming through the leaves from the other side. They were surrounded by water. It also smelled like the Great Lake, one of the destinations of the river that ran through Carl's city, but of course many lakes smell like that. It brought back memories of small sailing barges in long gone days, girls in summer clothes and promises and the smell of flowers. But there was no time for that now.

Then they went into the trees on a path that led to a large white summer residence, a 1950s design that summoned images from tabloid magazines, photographs of long forgotten movie stars in their summer clothes, parading their impeccable green lawn.

Inside the house he was tied to a chair in a large living room. There were windows in almost every direction, but the view from the lake was largely obstructed by a row of rhododendrons, fully matured. You could hide an elephant in these bushes and never know it existed until it trumpeted. The room was empty but for a table and chairs, curtains and a couch facing the rhododendrons, plus a small table with a telephone on it.

"Listen carefully," said the guy with the Bono mask. "Thanks to you a horror scenario has come true. The whole thing is utterly preposterous. I laughed when I heard you say it, but I can assure you I am not laughing now. You have planted an idea in our parents' minds, like a true hypnotist, and you are going to remove that idea before it does any real harm to anyone." He pointed at the phone.

Carl felt the ropes around his wrists. He thought feverishly. This was an ordinary summer residence phone, connected to a landline. That could be good. What if he could call the police from this location and ask them to trace the call, without asking it? Perhaps if he got through to lieutenant Carlsberg and hinted in a certain way. But the two masked men were standing there, looking at him. They were obviously not going to let him push any buttons here.

"I have no idea what you bonobos are talking about," said Pappas.

The Bill Gates character picked up the phone and held a finger at the buttons, ready to start dialing.

"You, Mr. Radio Dick, Mr. Bizz Jockey, have suggested that filthy rich people should give away all of their money as a way of testing their children's love for them."

Carl laughed.

"You think that's funny? Well, my parents have converted to your point of view. And his parents too. They are already taking precautions to ditch their billions and leave us with nothing. And not just us, but several other people we know are in the same shit right now. And you are..."

"Listen, kiddo, I sympathize with your financial worries, but you are talking to the wrong man. You don't need me." Carl turned his face to the other guy. "Tell him he needs his mommy."

The blow on his jaw was hard, but considering the curse that came from underneath the Bono mask it was the hitman who was in the most pain.

"You are going to talk our parents out of his!"

Carl was perplexed. "What?"

"All my friends are having this same problem with you. They've all been complaining and shouting and threatening. It's not just us. There's a lot of young folk who are just getting into the good life, you know, and then you show up and raise this... This ISSUE. Why ruin perfect family relationships by asking these stupid questions? You shouldn't wake people up that way and cause problems. Now get on the phone with my father and talk him out of it. He's an influential man and his position on this must change for all to see."

The masks looked at each other.

"Wait a minute," said Carl, "Don't dial yet. What do you m... I mean this is silly! It was a joke. You don't seriously expect your parents to ditch a billion dollars because I said so? That's insane."

"OF COURSE IT'S INSANE! And it's not just 'a' billion, it's several."

"And even if they did, you should call a lawyer. You can sue your parents for this. I know a fine lawyer. Why not call him right now? What... What are you doing?"

The Bono guy had walked over to the dining table and came back with a chair, raised above his head. "I'm sick and tired of this, I'm not taking your shit anymore, you talk my parents out of it NOW or you..." He smashed the chair into the floor with such force that it lost all coherence at once and splintered. "You get on the phone now. We have everything to lose."

"Listen kids, walk away from this while you can. If I talk to your parents, that means I can identify you after this is all over. I mean... that's hardly the perfect crime now, is it?"

"You think we're stupid or something?"

"Absolutely."

"We have everything to loose. So you better believe it. The next chair is for you, Mr. Radio Dick."

Carl looked at the other guy, the one with the Bill Gates mask, the one who didn't do much of the talking. "Be smart about this."

Bill Gates' response was not very promising. He just shrugged.

The Bono started to dial a number. "If you don't convince the man on the phone that his idea is stupid, we're going to use the gun on your knee."

===

They stood at the outskirts of the city, overlooking the Great Lake. Right in front of them was the pier the mysterious caller had talked about. The place was deserted.

"That is probably very normal on a Saturday afternoon, when it's cold and there's a wind blowing," said Don.

"Wait a minute, that sounds good," said Neil Kalen, who had driven his own car to the harbor. He had been calling Hitomi continuously to find out if there was any news about Carl. When he heard they were going to the harbor he joined them immediately. Now he took a small Moleskine from his jeans jacket and dotted down a few words. "Never skip a good song lyric idea," he said as he put it away, as Hitomi and Don looked on, stupefied.

"Can we get serious here?" said Hitomi. "The last location of Carl's cell phone was on that pier. It's obvious he took off from here, across the water."

"By seaplane or by speedboat, that's the question," said Don. "And I still think it sucks that you won't tell us where you're getting this information."

"No planes here," said Hitomi with authority. "Take my word for it. He's on a boat."

"It's a big lake," said Neil. He had a dreamy look on his face as he looked across the water.

"Yeah, it's great," said Don.

"We need one of these speedboats to check out the nearest islands," said Neil.

"I don't know," Hitomi protested. "This makes no sense whatsoever. Why would Carl go onto the lake? He's not the sailing kinda guy. He likes to sit by the shore and look across the water, not go on it."

"You know him that well?" said Neil.

"Well enough."

The pier was not a single pier, but a construction with many sidewalks, and many sailing boats and speedboats. Somewhere out there someone was shouting. They couldn't hear what was being shouted, but it drew their attention.

"Wait a minute," said Hitomi. Then she started running towards the pier, towards the shouting.

Neil ran after her. Don stood there looking for a moment, then followed, looking around him to see if no one was watching. Suddenly he felt ridiculous, chasing an imaginary crime. They would soon be exposed to the world as being naive adolescents and a troupe of ridiculous clowns. Clowns, he thought, were the scariest bunch around.

By the time he reached the scene there was a fight going on between Hitomi and a young man he didn't recognize immediately, though his face was familiar to him. Hitomi and the young man were shouting at each other, waving their arms, pointing fingers at each other. Neil tried to calm them down, but to no avail. In his stride, Don grabbed a bucket from the deck of a sailing barge and threw the contents — it was half filled with water — at Hitomi and the young man. That pretty much ended the screaming. It was precisely at that moment that Don remembered who the young man was. He was Moon Afficionades. His camouflage outfit could stand the water, but his sunglasses had fallen off. The young man bent over and picked them up.

"Dammit Don Lech Wozniak, why do always have to be

such a dick?" said Hitomi, but her anger was gone. She sounded like someone about to give up.

"This is my free Saturday. I hate it when my time is wasted. Let's get this over with. Please?"

"Tell him," said Hitomi.

The young man hesitated. "Why him? He's just a tech nerd. And he just wasted a perfectly good suit that his insurance is obviously not covering."

The look that Hitomi shot him was enough to convince him.

Fifteen

The Bono had left with the gun. The experience had enraged him and he had left the house, probably to cool off in the garden. Carl could see him pass through the rhododendrons towards the lake, shaking fists and apparently talking to himself. He had taken off the ridiculous singer's mask, but in the early twilight the back of the young man's head in the distance gave away no clues about his identity. Perhaps the man was Moon Afficionades, perhaps not.

They had not succeeded at making a single phone call. They had tried for three-quarters of an hour to call, apparently, both men's parents. All they got was voicemail blah blah. Finally Carl had said that all filthy rich were either still on the golf course where one doesn't take phone calls because that's downright impolite or they were takin' a shower after golf or they were already at the first cocktail party where the music's too loud to hear your cell phone. What finally tipped the Bono mask over the edge was Carl's remark that their fathers could also be fucking their mistresses at this hour, of course.

So there he sat and twilight was setting in and things were not looking good. So he thought about famous movies he'd seen, movies with the escapist acrobatics of famous movie stars. It occurred to him there was only one thing one could try. The thing he'd seen a thousand times. He was now guarded by the least aggressive of his two kidnappers, that helped.

"Hey man, I need to go to the john."

The young man with the Bill Gates mask sighed. Without making comments he untied Carl. Then he pointed to the door and said: "It's in the hall."

Carl started walking. The masked guy followed him closely.

"My partner's outside with a gun," he said, "and we're on an island. So don't get any funny ideas."

Carl went into the main hall and entered the toilet. Before closing the door he saw that the Gates character waited in the living room doorway.

The toilet was quite large. There was a seat of course, but also a hand-wash basin with soap and towels and a large mirror. Everything was squeaky clean. Whoever this house belonged to, his presence here would not remain undetected for very long. A cleaner would show up within days, no doubt about that.

But right now Carl like to think that minutes mattered more than days. So he opened the large stained glass window. He hadn't expected it to open, so when it did, that shocked him. But there was no one in sight. The lawn lay undisturbed at his right and before him. At his left were the rhododendrons and trees. If he got out he would be undercover of the leaves within a few seconds. The upcoming dusk would do the rest for him. He'd be hidden in the dark within a few moments.

"You deal with your own parents' lunacy," he murmured as he climbed out the window. He closed it behind him, although while he did that it felt like a pointless act. Then he bent over and ran to the trees. A rushing sound accompanied him as he plunged into the bushes. He kept running for dozens of meters and then he stood still. It was a lot darker here, night had almost fallen. The lake had to be right in front of him. He heard the sound of the waves breaking against the island.

As he stood there he heard another curse coming from behind him. So his head start was not going to very big after all. There was basically no advantage he could think of, other than the dark. He had to get to the boat or boats before they did, because that was probably the only way off this island. It was either that or back to the phone.

"We need to make a plan right now," said the Bono to the Gates. They had regrouped in the living room. "There are only two things that can go wrong. He can get away on the boat or he can make a phone call."

At that precise moment the phone on the small table rang.

"Don't tell me your dad's returning the call," said the Gates guy. "He'll want to know who's calling him from his summer house."

"It's not his summer house," snapped the Bono mask. "It's actually my mom's."

"That's academic, ain't it?"

"No it's not, but who cares right now?" said the Bono guy. "Leave it. We have to get to the boat and we have to get there fast. And get your mask back on."

They ran.

By now Moon Afficionades was driven into a corner on the deck of his speedboat. He had tried to get away from the trio by jumping onto his boat, but that had not worked out well. He was standing with his back to the cabin door, Hitomi right in front of him and the two men beside her. Hitomi kept stinging him in the chest with her finger. He liked strong women, which was why he had been attracted to the much older producer of The Boardroom in the first place, but right now he felt there was too much force being applied.

"If you know even the slightest detail about the disappearance of Carl Pappas, Moon, I swear you are going to regret it if you do not confess right here and right now."

"She works the bench at the gym," said Don. He relished the opportunity to talk about Hitomi's physique, and her supposed six-pack in particular. "And she works hard for the money too."

For once Hitomi did not try to shut him up. "Well, Moon? Where's Carl?"

"Step back, dammit," said Moon. "Do I look like a criminal to you, Hitomi? Step back and give me some room to explain."

So they stepped back, but only a little bit. They watched as Moon turned to open the cabin door and then put the key in the ignition. Finally he turned to them again.

"I got a call from a couple of friends of mine. I know they were extremely pissed by The Boardroom show I was on. You know, the silly stuff Mr. Pappas said about rich folks getting rid of their wealth."

"Yeah yeah," said Hitomi, "I've heard quite enough of that. It was just a show. What about your friends?"

"They were making plans to go to Mr. Pappas in person and talk to him and persuade him to take back his words on live radio, or something."

"This is getting dumber by the minute," laughed Neil Kalen. He sat down on the bench that circled the open air cockpit.

"And you think they got to him?" asked Hitomi, stepping forward again.

"Jesus," whispered Don.

"They called me an hour ago. They said they did something stupid and needed my help. They're on one of the islands over there, it's a private place of one of my friends' parents."

"You think they took Carl there."

"Jesus I hope not. If that's the case I'd rather stay out of it."

"If I recall you were pretty angry at Carl yourself," said Don.

"I am angry at my parents. Carl can say whatever he wants. It's a free world."

Then Neil Kalen jumped up. "Enough of the chit chat and radio ga-ga. If Carl is on the lake we have to get going. You, boys, loosen the mooring ropes. You girl, hold on tight." He stepped forward, grabbed the steering wheel and turned the key that Moon had already inserted.

"Now wait a minute," said Moon, but it was too late.

Don had thrown the two mooring ropes off the boat and Neil pushed the throttle forward. The engine roared.

Hitomi grabbed Neil's waist right before falling. Moon fell into the cockpit, cursing. The boat lifted its nose and sped away from the harbor at an increasing speed.

"Carl we're coming, hang in there buddy!" shouted Neil. "We're bringing money and muscles!"

"Who is this guy?" hissed Moon from the bottom of the ship.

But there was no answer and he had to watch his new girlfriend holding the waist of a tall hippie at the helm of his ship. Then he looked around and noticed that the sound engineer had disappeared off the rear of the boat altogether.

===

A gunshot rang out in the night. It was a single shot and it echoed across the water.

They are standing by the speedboat, Carl thought. He was in the bushes, in the interior of some huge rhododendron and by now it was evident that getting away by boat was not an option.

"Mr. Radio Dick? We know you're right there in the bushes. You are not going to get in the boat. But you may get shot if you stay in the bushes. Get that, Mr. Smooth Talker? I am going to fire this gun randomly into the rhododendrons unless you come out now. I will count to twenty, so let's hear it."

That was the Bono mask talking, no doubt. But Carl wasn't hanging around to test the man's resilience. He was obviously bluffing, because firing bullets at random would bring him nothing but an empty gun real soon. But Carl was not going to take chances with guns, so he backed off quietly and made his way back to the house and then to the other side of the island.

There was nothing to be seen there. As gunshots sounded from the other side of the house he looked at the shore of the island. It was nothing more than rhododendrons suddenly opening up to a wooden shielding leading down into the water. And the water looked black.

Behind him the gunshots kept sounding and they seemed to be coming his way.

And again the water looked black and uninviting. If no one was coming to his rescue then there was no point hanging around on this island. He wondered if he could do a show on private islands and their economic impact. Plenty of people owned islands. Hell, even Marlon Brando had had an island once. So it could be kinda innarestin'.

Another gunshot reverberated, followed by a whistling sound close to him. That did it. Carl bent over and slid into the water. It was cold, but not cold enough to stop him. As soon as he was in the water he started to swim away from the island, quietly, without making any splashing noises. Right in front of him was the city, but it was far away. It was, in fact, barely visible.

===

Water spat up from the front of the speedboat. Its bow was hammering the surface of the Great Lake. By now it was completely dark and if there was an island there was no way of knowing where it was.

Suddenly Hitomi grabbed the throttle and pulled it back. The ship slowed down immediately and flattened itself on the water, the bow down again.

"What?" said Neil.

"This is my boat," said Moon from the bench behind them. "And are you aware of the fact that your sound guy fell of the boat?"

"WHAT!" shouted Hitomi. "NOW you tell us? We have to get back right now. But not so fast, Neil. You could hit anything. What if you sail right over Carl?"

But Moon got up, jumped to the wheel, pushing Neil Kalen aside. "Allow me Mr. Hippie Superstar." He pushed some buttons and revved up the engine again. A powerful light switched on at the front of the boat. "One of you go out there and point the light at the lake right in front of us. you're right, indeed I don't want to be sailing right into a swimmer's ass."

Sixteen

"It's your commerce guru, your buddy, your money maker, your bizz jockey and he's going down in the Great Lake, people," mumbled Carl. He was feeling weak. Things were not moving in the right direction tonight.

The shots from the island behind him had faded a long time ago. That had been hopeful. Another hopeful thing had led to nothing. He had seen a speedboat approaching from the city in the distance. But then it had stopped all of a sudden, turned on a huge searchlight and returned the way it came.

That had been fifteen minutes ago. And to make things worse he now heard the sounds of a speedboat coming from the direction of the island. These idiots with there masks on were coming for him again. What were the odds of them finding him in this sea of black?

Or worse: what would happen if they didn't find him? By now Carl realized that the main shore of the Great Lake was too far for him. He was not going to make it swimming. So he stayed were he was, floating, looking back and forth to see which of the two boats would show up first.

From the island the speedboat approached, though not directly in Carl's direction. It made large circles in the water. The other speedboat had disappeared in the direction of the city. He wondered why the hell he hadn't just agreed to talk to the fathers of these kids? The whole thing felt like a stupid mistake that the older and wiser should have taken care of for the younger generation.

Too late now, he thought. Now he had to make sure he was seen. Yet how on earth could he draw attention in the dark when the waves were engulfing a drowning man's voice? He started to fade, cold to the bone. He saw shimmers of light dancing up and down in front of him. Yet he did not realize it was the speedboat from the island, with two men on it who had shoved their masks down under their chins, looking for their fugitive hostage with a pocket lamp. The light was not that strong at all, but after a couple of circles they spotted the floating bizz jockey, who was about to descend to deeper waters. They pulled the boat alongside Carl Pappas, grabbed him together and pulled him aboard. By then he had already lost consciousness. After they'd laid him out on the bench in the cockpit the Bono guy hit the gas and the boat sped back, disappearing into the darkness.

By the time they docked again at the island pier, Carl started to wake up. They put him on his feet and held him up under his armpits as they walked onto the island, through the bushes towards the lawn and then onto the house, lit by nothing but the moon and the flashlight one of the men held. Carl tried to regain control of the situation — if he'd ever had any control over the situation to begin with.

"I-I-I... I'll t-talk t-to your d-dads...," he stammered, his teeth rattling. "I've thought things over, you s-see."

"That's funny," said the Bono guy. "That's very funny. I'm laughing. You hear? Hah hah."

They grew more violent as they entered the house, firming their grip on their guest, speeding up their walk and then throwing him into the couch by the telephone.

"We're going to start all over again," said the Bono guy.

The phone rang.

The young men looked at each other. It occurred to Carl that he could now see their faces proper, and suddenly they were aware of their nakedness, and they hurriedly put their masks back on. But they had exposed themselves long enough for Carl to recognize William Hackensack the third as the man impersonating Bono. The Gates guy remained unknown to him.

The Bono picked up the phone, probably a reflex caused by the general confusion.

The Gates shouted something, perhaps to warn him, but it was too late.

"Hello?" said the Bono into the telephone, beginning to realize his mistake and trying to remain anonymous.

Someone started to shout at the other end of the line, much to the horror of the Bono, or William, who just stood there nodding. Then he turned to the Gates guy and said: "It's my dad and he's... He's on his way over."

The Bill Gates mask showed no response to this message, but the attached body definitely did. He turned from the scene and started running towards the door.

"Jerry, you..." shouted William, but he stopped in mid-sentence and with his mouth wide open listened to the roar of a helicopter approaching the house, hovering over the lawn, its searchlights bombarding the living room and blinding them all.

Carl got up and as he stood next to the stupefied William he looked onto the lawn that was now flooded with light from two helicopters hanging right over it. The grass was now busy with people. He saw the silhouette of the Bill Gates guy disappearing into the rhododendrons, he saw Hitomi and Don and Neil and Moon backing away towards the house, to get out of the way of the helicopters as they were descending.

Then Carl grabbed the mask and yanked it off William's face — only to find himself staring right into the barrel of the young man's gun.

"Take it easy, take it real easy, we're going this way."

"Give it up, son. Where will you run to now?"

"Don't patronize me, I got the gun. Over there, there's a back door."

William pushed the bizz jockey towards a screen door at the end of the room, kicked it open with his foot and next thing Carl new he was running away from the house, the barrel of the gun stinging his back.

"Over here!" he shouted.

"Damn you!" hissed William and he jumped on Carl's back, closing his mouth by putting one hand on his mouth.

As a result, they fell. Next thing Carl knew, he was lying flat on the ground, his mouth covered by his assaulter's hand. The kid lay on top of him, the gun against his head. It was very dark. No one had heard them. They would search the place, obviously, but Carl wanted to get this over with before

William got a chance to do more damage.

Then he had an idea. His right hand was free, so he moved it up slowly till he reached the kid's jacket. He felt the pocket light. With very delicate movements of his hand he pulled the light out of the pocket. William was not moving, he was breathing heavily and paying attention to the noises coming from the other wide of the house, obviously thinking hastily about what to do next.

Carl moved the pocket light around in his hand till he had the firmest possible grip and then he turned his arm and slammed the metal object against William's skull with as much force as he could muster. The blow was not powerful to render the man unconscious, but it had yielded enough momentum to throw him entirely off guard, let go of Carl's mouth as well as the gun.

With sheer willpower Carl raised himself on his arms and threw the body off him, at the same time raising his voice to start the loudest mischief a radio master was capable of.

By then the helicopter rotor blades had slowed down enough for him to be heard this time. A crowd of people came running around the house. All the people he had seen, but also other people, people in suits, people in uniforms, a whole swarm. Up front was Bill Hackensack the second. As Carl lost consciousness the last thing he saw was the billionaire coming down on his knees towards his son, and he wondered whether the man was kneeling in anger or in fear.

Seventeen

The city lay unmoved beneath the windows of Carl Pappas' office. He sat there looking from his chair, trying to raise a clear thought about all that had happened, from deep within, but nothing came. Tonight's show had been prepared properly, nothing could go wrong, but he felt something was missing. His girlfriend had returned from abroad and would come to the studio later, to go out and have dinner with him. His wounds had healed enough over the course of the Sunday and the Monday to free him of pain. But still, something was missing. He had not been able to come up with the right line for tonight's show to sum it all up. He had briefed Job Messner, his staff writer, his soundbite champion, but nothing had come up that satisfied him. Of course he had not told Job about that; the man had come up with enough other lines that were funny or to the point or insightful.

He heard a noise and looked to his side. Hitomi Sakamoto was standing there, looking out the window too. How long had she been there?

"If you want to smoke and confess, better go to Don," said Carl.

Hitomi did not reply. She kept her eyes on the city. In all these years of working together Pappas had never been able to really figure her out. She was very involved in everything, even in parts of his personal life, but when push came to shove she did things in a silent way. She could raise her voice against Don and Phil and against powerful guests from politics or business, but in the end, when it really mattered, she would simple stare right into a man's eyes and force her will upon him. And now, it seemed she was bringing a message across, but Carl couldn't figure out what that message was.

"You never explained to me why a woman like you is a Liberace fan," said Carl.

Hitomi laughed. She looked sideways, at Carl. "I never said I was a Liberace fan, you crazy man."

"But you know who Liberace was, woman. You see, you send messages without words and that is very confusing. How am I supposed to know what you mean when you don't talk? Perhaps you're sorry for getting involved with that rich kid? Or perhaps you're sorry for steering his speedboat into a rock? They told me you guys jump onto the island without getting your feet wet and that his boat stood vertically in the water. Don't worry, the kid can afford a new one."

"Carl Evangelos Pappas, you talk too much. I'm just standing here." She gave him another smile, a soft sort of friendship thing. Then she walked out.

"Liberace!" Carl yelled after her.

Don had been putting up a Liberace piece a couple of times and he had seen a look on Hitomi's face then. Well, he thought, she hadn't denied it. If one worked with Hitomi

Sakamoto long enough, perhaps she would reveal some more of her inner self. But the Moon character was out of her life, and perhaps she needed some form of confirmation from the bizz jockey.

But perhaps it was all bullshit and she had just been waiting for the final moments to pass, the final moments before tonight's broadcast took off.

And so it took off. Carl was glad to be back in time. He had made it. And there was some unfinished business for him there.

The opening tune blasted its way to the audience, then taken over by the voice of WCBN Radio: "It's eleven o'clock. The city is dark, but the fire burns. It burns in the offices. It burns on Wall Street. It burns in the City. It burns on the Bund. It burns in Dubai. It burns in the factories and power plants. And it burns within us. Because we are the business and we all need redemption. This is the hour of delusion and today's truth. This is The Boardroom. Here is your prophet, the buddy and the bodyguard of every CEO, the Don Juan of every business babe. Here is the world's one and only bizz jockey. Here is your BJ: Carl Pappas!"

"Quite rightly so, people. If your kids ever blame you for something, let's hope it's for losing your money or for giving it away. Because I can tell from personal experience it's a lot easier to deal with kids who are pissed off about money than it is to deal with kids who are pissed off because their parents don't love them. So once again I welcome you, men and women of the business, to The Boardroom, where just like any other day we ask ourselves: where do we stand? If you know the answer, you may call now. But don't take this lightly; you may end up alone in the middle of the economic ocean and find out you're all alone and the shore is too far away to swim. It's a cruel world out there, people, it's full of sharks and you know what? The big question is whether the shark is coming for you... or whether you yourself are the shark. Figure that one out. For your sake, I hope at least you care. And here's our first caller. This is Carl Pappas in The Boardroom, can I help you?"

"Hi, this is Moon Afficionades."

Carl could feel the eyes of Hitomi suddenly open even wider than they already were. He thought he heard a sudden silence beyond the glass where Don and Hitomi were.

"Moon. You are about the last person I expected."

He looked at the sound booth. Don was smiling at him. Hitomi looked without looking, a blank stare.

"I want to thank you," said Moon. "Thanks to you, my parents wanted to do away with all their assets."

"So it seems. I wouldn't thank me if I were you, man. I make one crazy comment on a person's wealth and then this happens. That sucks."

"Not just yet. I had them subpoenaed and now everything is frozen until the case goes to court."

"That could take years. Very clever, Moon. Now tell me, young man, does being a billionaire's son give you an edge with the ladies?"

"I beg your pardon?"

"You are so polite," said Carl. "Do women fall for your good looks or your money?"

"Who cares? Do women fall for your dick or your fame, Mr.

Pappas?"

"Tough words, young man. Listen, how far are you willing to go? Has it occurred to you that if you had just said to your parents, mom, dad, I love you no matter what you do, they might have called the whole damned thing off? Has that occurred to you? Has it occurred to you that by taking them to court you've actually proven their worst fear to be true? That you only love them for their money?"

"You suck, Carl Pappas. And to answer your question: I'm willing to go very, very far."

Carl raised his hand like a referee, getting Don's attention. He was about to make the "cut the line" gesture. "Are you willing to die for it?"

"If that means I die rich: yes."

"It's not worth it, son. Trust me," said Carl. He made the gesture. The call was terminated. "Looks like we haven't heard the last of the Afficionades yet, people. I must say, I had my doubts about my own words, but by now I'm starting to see the light. Before I leave you for some messages and before we get on with more important business at hand, I ask you this: how can you die rich if you've sold out on love? How exactly is that a rich death? You tell me. But I warn you, you're going to have a tough time convincing the bizz jockey."

On the other side of the glass, Hitomi Sakamoto raised her hands in a silent applause.

***

Request from the author

Thank you for reading this Radio Detective adventure. I hope you enjoyed it and will be willing to write a review on the online platform of your choice. Making that extra effort is greatly appreciated by other readers... and of course by me. Thank you.

I hope you and I stay connected through Twitter, Facebook, Google+, Pinterest or my free email newsletter. I'll make sure you'll stay tuned.

Have a good evening/night/day!

M.H. Vesseur

Twitter @MHVesseur

Facebook www.facebook.com/MHVesseur

Subscribe to M.H. Vesseur's mailing list on www.mhvesseur.com

About the author

M.H. Vesseur has written many short stories for literary magazines in The Netherlands, Belgium, Canada and the U.S.A. He was awarded for the best debut with his first story. In his radio detective series about Carl Pappas he has now written and published the seven short crime novels *CEO Groupie*, *Die Rich*, *Tax Me If You Can*, *Acid Asset*, *Nosedive*, *Power Play* and *Blood Border*. The radio detective's producer Hitomi Sakamoto now stars in her own series, which begins with *North*. M.H. Vesseur also published the novel *Lemniscate*, a collection of literary short stories called *Allusions* and his outlook on the super economy *Burning Neil Armstrong*. M.H. Vesseur is an awarded advertising copywriter. He lives in the forests of The Netherlands.

www.mhvesseur.com

Novels and ebooks by M.H. Vesseur

More information on:
www.mhvesseur.com/publications

Allusions (short story collection)
North (The Hitomi Files: 1)
Blood Border (a Radio Detective novel)
Power Play (a Radio Detective novel)
Nosedive (a Radio Detective novel)
Acid Asset (a Radio Detective novel)
Tax Me If You Can (a Radio Detective novel)
Die Rich (a Radio Detective novel)
CEO Groupie (a Radio Detective novel)
Beloved Stalker
Babyface Junkie
In Snuff Park
Sketches Of A Worldwide Christo And Jeanne-Claude
Narcissist Guru
Territory Game

Short stories by M.H. Vesseur

ALLUSIONS

Glimpses of tomorrow await you in this collection. The ultimate amusement park will offer you death. Everlasting youth will take you to the point of no return. The artificial landscape will fill you with joy if it doesn't scare the living daylights out of you. The Narcissist Guru will show you your many selves. There is the ultimate work of art that will change the planet and the old vaudeville star who is still being stalked. And finally, the coming of the super economy will haunt your dreams. This collection contains the short stories • In Snuff Park • Babyface Junkie • Narcissist Guru • Sketches of a Worldwide Christo and Jeanne-Claude • Territory Game • Beloved Stalker • Burning Neil Armstrong.

Available in The Hitomi Files by M.H. Vesseur

NORTH

Man should fear only one enemy

The only enemy who has the capacity to remove all of mankind from the earth, is the virus. Imagine the worst of them all, a true 21st century killer. It lies dormant in the remote laboratory of a pharmaceutical giant whose hopes of making billions off a vaccine somewhere in the future throw a dark shadow ahead. Then Hitomi Sakamoto, the hard boiled radio producer who's on a rough vacation in the wild nature of the north, stumbles upon this dark secret. She is drawn into a final battle between ruthless scientists, a greedy corporation, desperate but dangerous environmental activists, a cold-hearted assassin and... a manmade virus that longs to escape.

Hitomi Sakamoto first appeared in the Radio Detective novels by

M.H. Vesseur. Immediately popular for her iron work ethics and razorsharp tongue, Hitomi outgrew her boss (radio detective Carl Pappas) and now steps out of his shadow, into her very own adventure.

Available in the radio detective series by M.H. Vesseur

CEO GROUPIE - A radio detective novel

One night three live guests join Carl Pappas on his radio show The Boardroom: two CEOs and a woman who calls herself: "the CEO Groupie". When the mysterious woman reveals the existence of a secret call girl organization for CEOs and subsequently disappears a couple of days later, the bizz jockey engages on a search. What happened to the CEO Groupie and what are the other two guests up to? Together with his radio team — his producer Hitomi Sakamoto and his sound engineer Don Wozniak — Carl Pappas sets out to deal with this.

Available in the radio detective series by M.H. Vesseur

TAX ME IF YOU CAN - A radio detective novel

Carl Pappas, the bizz jockey, is cooking up a real shocker: during a live broadcast of his popular business talk radio show "The Boardroom" he plans to reveal secrets about tax dodging practices around the globe. In the middle of the preparations he and his producer Hitomi Sakamoto face unexpected trouble. Who is trying to shut the Bizz Jockey up in this quiet country under the tropical sun? Is it the local military junta? Is it the business community? Or is the sun finally getting to Carl Pappas' head?

Available in the radio detective series by M.H. Vesseur

ACID ASSET - A radio detective novel

Carl Pappas, the bizz jockey, is feeling good about the prospects of environment-friendly plastics he's discussing on his radio show "The Boardroom". But as he soon finds out there's something not right with the company behind it. Can the bizz jockey protect a lonely scientist against the schemes of a large corporation that smells money? Or will he be unable to stop a revolutionary asset from becoming really acidic? Buckle up for a race against arsonists, corporate crime, dogs, bullets and a dangerous industrial zone in the middle of a blizzard, softened only by some real team spirit.

Also available in the radio detective series

NOSEDIVE - A radio detective novel

When a large corporation is struck by a cripling strike among its workers and an apparent terrorist attack on its factory, bizz jockey Carl Pappas steps forward to offer his public support. But as he soon finds out, there's more to the picture than meets the eye. Why is the owner hiding in her large mansion? What happened in her youth that is threatening her after all these years? It's a job for the radio detective — and this time around his boss gives an unexpected hand.

Available in the radio detective series by M.H. Vesseur

POWER PLAY - A radio detective novel

The death of an environmental activist brings bizz jockey and unofficial "radio detective" Carl Pappas to the quiet island of Islasol. Everything seems to be OK with the local National Park and the wind turbine park in the heart of it.

But Carl and his team soon find out you can't take anything on face value. Below the surface of an environment friendly enterprise lies a darker secret. It's time for the radio detective to unravel the local secrets of wind energy, assisted by his producer Hitomi and a new, unlikely ally.

Available in the radio detective series by M.H. Vesseur

BLOOD BORDER - A radio detective novel

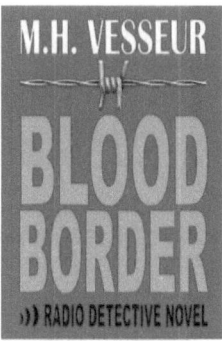

The inhumanity of human trafficking is forcing the radio detective to make a stand. So in the midst of politics and public outrage, Carl Pappas and his team infiltrate the trafficking cartel of a man known as The Clown. But there is nothing funny about it, for the radio detective soon finds himself in the lion's den, a place crowded with former narcotics traffickers and their violent ways. Will they be able to do something about the screaming injustice of immigration or will they become prey themselves?

<<<<>>>>